Bello:

hidden talent rediscovered!

Bello is a digital only imprint of Pan Macmillan, established to breathe new life into previously published, classic books.

At Bello we believe in the timeless power of the imagination, of good story, narrative and entertainment and we want to use digital technology to ensure that many more readers can enjoy these books into the future.

We publish in ebook and Print on Demand formats to bring these wonderful books to new audiences.

About Bello:

www.panmacmillan.com/imprints/bello

About the author:

www.panmacmillan.com/author/andrewgarve

Andrew Garve

Andrew Garve is the pen name of Paul Winterton (1908–2001). He was born in Leicester and educated at the Hulme Grammar School, Manchester and Purley County School, Surrey, after which he took a degree in Economics at London University. He was on the staff of *The Economist* for four years, and then worked for fourteen years for the *London News Chronicle* as reporter, leader writer and foreign correspondent. He was assigned to Moscow from 1942–5, where he was also the correspondent of the BBC's Overseas Service.

After the war he turned to full-time writing of detective and adventure novels and produced more than forty-five books. His work was serialized, televised, broadcast, filmed and translated into some twenty languages. He is noted for his varied and unusual backgrounds – which have included Russia, newspaper offices, the West Indies, ocean sailing, the Australian outback, politics, mountaineering and forestry – and for never repeating a plot.

Andrew Garve was a founder member and first joint secretary of the Crime Writers' Association.

Andrew Garve

THE CASE OF ROBERT QUARRY

First published in 1972 by Collins

This edition published 2012 by Bello
an imprint of Pan Macmillan, a division of Macmillan Publishers Limited
Pan Macmillan, 20 New Wharf Road, London N1 9RR
Basingstoke and Oxford
Associated companies throughout the world

www.panmacmillan.com/imprints/bello
www.curtisbrown.co.uk

ISBN 978-1-4472-1520-2 EPUB
ISBN 978-1-4472-1519-6 POD

A CIP catalogue record for this book is available from the British Library.

PART ONE

Chapter One

Detective Chief Superintendent Joseph Burns made a graceful cast and dropped the Greenwell's Glory on to the fragment of newspaper forty feet away. If the lawn had been a pool, a trout could have been lurking there. Burns's twelve-year-old grandson stood by, watching the action of the expert with intent approval.

'Right,' Burns said, 'now you try again. And remember to let the rod do the work. Make it *bend*.'

The boy tried again, with his own rod—the birthday rod that his grandfather had given him. This time his fly landed within a couple of yards of the newspaper.

'That's much better,' Burns said. 'You're still jerking a little on the back cast but you're beginning to get the knack. How are the muscles?'

'Aching a bit,' the boy said, with a grin.

'They're bound to, to start with—but they'll soon ease up. And you're doing fine, Tim. A couple of hours' practice a week, and you'll be a creditable fly fisherman by the end of next season.' Burns paused to re-light his pipe. He had the relaxed air of a man whose cares would soon be behind him. His appearance was benign. With his balding head fringed at sides and back by curling grey hair, his bushy grey moustache, his plump jowls and his expression of wise good humour, he looked more like an elderly cherub than a policeman. And, today, a particularly contented cherub. Instructing an ardent young angler-to-be in the garden of his Nottinghamshire home was a most satisfying way of spending a fine October Sunday morning. Almost as satisfying as being actually on a river bank . . .

Fishing—and especially dry fly fishing—was not less a passion with Burns because his demanding profession had given him only rare opportunities to indulge in it. It was a pastime that wholly suited his temperament and his needs. It required close study and concentration; the habit of attention and observation; foresight and intelligent planning; self-control and endurance. It afforded incomparable delights—whether the quiet satisfaction of putting a dry fly perfectly to a trout in a difficult place or the supreme excitement of playing a fish that contested every inch of the line. It could be enjoyed in beautiful surroundings—sometimes tranquil, sometimes dramatic, but always a welcome contrast to the sordidness and squalor that a policeman so often had to face in his job. And, even if a day ended with an empty basket, there were always agreeable associations to look back on . . .

'Right, young Tim,' he said, 'let's have another go, shall we?'

In the kitchen, his wife, Alice, was lightening the chore of washing up by pleasurably watching their progress through the open window. As a girl, Alice had been a pretty redhead; slim and vivacious; now, in her late fifties, her short curly hair was whiter than white, but—in Buras's eyes, at least—the prettiness was still there. Nor had she put on any weight; her waist was still what it had been at nineteen. Small bones and delicate features gave her an appearance of fragility which was wholly misleading, for in fact she was wiry and tough. She had enjoyed excellent health throughout an unusually active life; she had produced three strapping sons, and she was still full of energy. Burns had found her to be the best of companions in the outdoor life he loved.

As she put the last of the breakfast things in the rack to drain, the telephone rang in Burns's work-room. Alice dried her hands and went to answer it. 'Four two nine eight seven,' she said briskly. 'Oh, good morning . . . Yes, we're fine, thank you . . . Yes, of course I'll tell him.' She hurried back to the kitchen and called through the window. 'Telephone, Joe.' As her husband came in she said, 'It's Ivison. I expect it's about your presentation.'

Burns went through to his room and picked up the receiver. 'Morning, sir.'

'Morning, Joe,' the chief constable said. 'I apologize for disturbing you, but we're in rather a spot. I've just had word that Robert Quarry's been murdered.'

'Really?' Burns said, after only the shortest of pauses. 'Where, sir?'

'Heavens, man, doesn't anything ever startle you . . .? A few miles outside Lowark. His body's been found in the boot of a car. I'd like you to take charge.'

For the first time in his professional life, Burns demurred at an instruction. 'You haven't forgotten, sir, that I'm being put out to grass in just over a week?'

'I know that, Joe—but at least you can make a start on the case. It's clearly a job for a senior man, and you're the only one available. Bryant and Ellis are up to their eyes, and Pickering's still down with pleurisy. And you may find you can clear the whole thing up in a week . . . It could be the last big feather in your cap.'

Burns grunted. 'Well, I'll do it, of course, sir. Can I have Sergeant Ryder?'

'I knew you'd ask that. He's already on his way to the scene.'

'And Williams?'

'If you need him. You can have anyone who's free, do anything you like. I want results, that's all.'

'Very well, sir. Where's the place?' Burns reached for an inch-to-the-mile of the district and spread it out.

'Take B 1184 out of Lowark—the Illingham road. At four miles you cross a stone bridge over a stream. Immediately beyond the bridge there's a track through a wood on the left.'

'I've got it,' Burns said.

'You'll find the car some way along the track. I've alerted Carson and Bell—they'll be joining you later.'

'Very good,' Burns said. 'I'll be over there in half an hour.'

He hung up, and went to tell Alice.

Burns had cultivated over the years an air of philosophic calm where his job was concerned. There were so many sudden developments in police work, so many sensations and crises and alarms, that a certain phlegm was necessary for health and sanity. Even murder—even the murder of a well-known figure—had to be taken coolly.

Alice's reaction was less professional. 'Robert Quarry!' she exclaimed. 'Good heavens, what a terrible thing!' She looked very shocked.

'Yes,' Burns said, methodically checking the contents of his murder bag. 'It'll be quite a responsibility.'

'It certainly will!' Her concern was of a different kind now. 'Well, I do think that's mean ... Giving you a big job like that when you've only a few more days to go.'

Burns smiled wryly. 'Ivison said it could be the last big feather in my cap.'

'You don't need more feathers. What does he think you are—a Red Indian?' Alice began to put the china away, the concern in her face deepening. 'Joe,' she said after a moment, 'it won't affect our holiday, will it?'

Burns raised his right hand. 'It won't, dear. I swear.'

'I shall hold you to that,' Alice said.

As he drove sedately along in his Ford Zephyr, bowler hat on head, murder bag beside him and emergency overnight case in the back, Burns recalled what he knew about the dead man and his activities.

Robert Quarry was an industrialist, chairman of a light engineering company named Crowther's which had a head office in London and some half-dozen factories scattered around the country. One of the factories, located at Lowark, made motor-car components. At this plant there had been, for the past six weeks, a bitter unofficial strike over the sacking of a shop steward. At Quarry's insistence, the Lowark management had taken a strong line. The three thousand workers had been laid off, the plant temporarily closed, and talks with the strike committee ended. There had been a succession of angry meetings and demonstrations outside the works, and some ugly clashes with the local police.

Quarry had been denounced by the militants as a tight-fisted capitalist, the workers' enemy, in a crescendo of abuse.

Without in the least pre-judging the matter, Burns wasn't entirely surprised that he had been murdered. As the Americans said, it figured.

One thing was very clear—this was going to be an important, a sensational case. It was certain to be reported prominently in the national newspapers. Quarry had been a big shot in the manufacturing world, an outstandingly dynamic figure—and the pressmen would come swarming into Lowark. They'd be wanting interviews, they'd be clamouring for quick results. They'd have the spotlight on the man in charge. There'd be a feathered cap, indeed, for success—but a cap with bells for failure. At any other time, Burns would have welcomed the challenge. But at this penultimate moment in his career, he was concerned much more about the trip to France that was scheduled to start on Wednesday week.

He and Alice had always had the desire to travel. They were by inclination open-air people, and within the narrow limits of Burns's annual holiday and slender purse they had followed their inclination. Year after year, when the boys were young, they had taken them on exciting and sometimes arduous expeditions—camping and fell-walking in the Lakes, climbing in Snowdonia, caravanning in the Highlands—with water and fishing always at hand. One and all, they had enjoyed themselves. Later, when the family had grown up and departed, Burns and Alice had begun to go abroad occasionally—but with time and money still short, these holidays had been little more than tentative sorties. Now, with Burns's coming retirement, an entirely new prospect had opened up. Time would be of no account—and to explore exotic places in a modest way would be hardly more expensive than to stay at home. So, with the aid of innumerable maps and guides, and with enormous shared enthusiasm, they had planned their first trip for the days of unlimited leisure. They would go first to the Dordogne—where the fishing was said to be excellent—and visit Lascaux and the great cavern of Padirac and the antiquities at Les Eyzies; and then they would work their way down to the warm south and explore Provence, which they'd dreamt and talked of doing for more than thirty years. That was the plan—and it would be carried out. The arrangements were made, the Dormobile was hired, the passage was booked—and there definitely wasn't going to be any postponement.

That being so, Burns thought, it was almost certain that someone else would have to take over the case in ten days' time. Which wasn't a very satisfactory state of affairs. Not that the murderer would benefit from a handover in mid-course—he wouldn't. One good detective could cope as well as another—or so Burns modestly believed. But from his own point of view it was unsatisfactory. He knew very well what might happen. Routine inquiries, tedious probing and no results for several days. Then, suddenly, an exciting break and an absorbing problem. If that was the way the case went, Burns was well aware that he'd want to see it through.

The ancient market town of Lowark was lively with traffic on this fine Sunday morning. Burns crossed the Trent, skirted the impressive ruins of the castle, threaded his way through the narrow streets, and turned off with relief along the minor road to Illingham. He had no difficulty in locating the opening in the wood beyond the stone bridge that Ivison had mentioned. The track was about twice the width of a car, overgrown with short grass and flanked on both sides by scrubby trees. He followed its winding course for a hundred yards or more before he came upon the police party. There was a radio patrol car, with a uniformed sergeant and constable; Detective-Sergeant Thomas Ryder with his Hillman; and, a little way beyond, a beige-coloured 3-litre Rover parked beside the track.

Burns said 'Good morning' to the uniformed men, both of whom he'd met. The sergeant, he recalled, was named Conway; the constable was Jim Pearce. Burns greeted Ryder with a smile and a friendly grasp of the arm.

The detective-sergeant was a complete contrast to Burns in almost every way. He was young, vigorous, darkly good-looking and—by the standards of the Force—trendily turned out His plain clothes were not nearly as plain as Burns's old-fashioned dark suit, and he had black sideboards reaching well down his cheeks in the transient fashion of the day. In temperament, too, he was very different from the superintendent. Burns was reflective, analytical, logical. Ryder was imaginative, an ideas man, ever ready to gallop away on a theory and see where it led. Burns had worked with him successfully on two murder cases and had found him a valuable foil to himself as well as an agreeable colleague. Ryder, for his part, had a profound respect for Burns, whose quiet and patient approach he had twice seen culminate in a sharp and deadly interrogation. Ryder's ranging ideas might bring a suspect to light, but there was no one like Burns to nail him. Sergeant and superintendent complemented each other like hand and glove.

Conway led the way to the Rover. The lid of the large boot was open, revealing the body of a middle-aged man, dressed in a grey tweed country suit. The body was lying on its right side in a hunched position, the legs drawn up to the stomach. The left arm was flung outwards, and protruded from the boot almost to the bumper. The face, with its pallid lips, glassy stare and dropped jaw, had the ugly look of death. Face and head were contused, and the side of the throat that was exposed by the angle of the head had a dark purple patch that also looked like heavy bruising. There was no sign of blood anywhere.

Burns said, 'Who decided it was Quarry?'

Pearce, the constable, spoke up. 'I recognized him, sir. I'd seen him several times at the factory.'

'Ah! And is this his car?'

'Yes, sir. The one he always drove.'

'Fair enough.' Burns turned to Conway. 'Right—put me in the picture, Sergeant, will you? Who found him, and when?'

Conway reported. 'A group of hikers came upon the car just before 9.30 this morning, sir. The boot lid was shut, but they saw an arm sticking out. One of them ran on till he found a house with a phone, and dialled the station. Constable Pearce and I arrived on the scene at 10 a.m. The hikers said they hadn't touched anything apart from lifting the boot lid to look inside, and closing it again.'

'Good—that's something . . .' Burns stood for a moment, eyeing the boot. Then he drew on a pair of gloves and carefully lowered the lid by its edges till it rested on the arm. Nearly a foot of arm protruded. He raised the lid again and tested the arm for stiffness. Rigor had begun to set in.

He stood back. 'What did he weigh, I wonder—a little over twelve stone? Quite a job getting that sort of dead weight into a boot.'

'You're right,' Ryder agreed. 'No joke at all. The sort of thing they do better in the movies than in real life. You get a shot of someone heaving at a body. Then, next shot, it's safely in.'

'The murderer could have had help, of course,' Burns said. He continued his investigation. The cadaver would be for the pathologist to examine, and he left it alone, concentrating on externals. The tip of a wallet showed at the dead man's breast pocket where the jacket had fallen open, and he extracted it and looked through its contents. There were eight five-pound notes and three singles; an RAC membership card; a driving licence and a gun licence; and a couple of credit cards. The licences and the cards were in the name of Robert Quarry, and the address was given as The Hillocks, Harpenden, Herts. There was also a letter, a brief note on a single sheet of paper without an envelope, dated December 4th of the previous year and, by its frayed appearance, much read. It ran:

Darling Robert,

It was such a wonderful, *wonderful* evening and I'm quite deliriously happy. I know it's silly to write when I'll be seeing you the day after tomorrow but it makes me feel near you just to write 'darling' and to say again 'I love you', as I do so desperately. I'm counting not just the hours but the *minutes* until Wednesday, and still pinching myself to make sure it's not just a dream and that after that we'll really be together all the time, for ever and ever. I love you so much, darling . . .

Your own
Alma

Burns passed the note to Ryder. Ryder looked at it, and pulled a face, and said, 'Sounds like she was just going to marry him. Only ten months ago, too. Poor woman!' Burns nodded, and took the note back, and replaced it carefully in the wallet, and the wallet in the jacket.

Then he turned his attention to the car. In the travel dust on the bonnet, the word BASTARD had been scrawled in rough capitals. Against a background of murder, it seemed a superfluous bit of *graffiti*. He opened one of the doors and looked inside. The interior of the car was wrecked. The passenger seat had been forced back and broken away from its mounting. The internal upholstery was ripped in several places, the front offside window was cracked, and the clock face was smashed. The clock had stopped at 2.31. Burns eyed it in a slightly jaundiced way, but didn't comment.

'Looks as though there was quite a punch-up,' Ryder said.

'Yes . . .'

'Quarry was a hefty bloke. I should think the murderer must have finished up with a few marks on him.'

'Yes,' Burns agreed. 'We'll bear it in mind.'

He walked slowly around the car, studying the ground. There were faint but unmistakable signs that the Rover had been reversed on the narrow track. It had come in from the road, and it had been turned so that it now pointed back towards the road. Burns stood looking at the tyre marks for some moments.

'Where does this track lead to?' he asked Conway.

'Nowhere very much, sir,' the sergeant said. 'It used to be the way to a farm, but the place has been derelict for years.' He pointed ahead. 'Just round the corner there, it narrows to an overgrown path.'

'There's no way through for a car?'

'No, sir, it's just a footpath. It comes out on the high road after a couple of miles. I don't think anyone uses it now except the odd hiker.'

'I see.' Burns looked back towards the bridge, which was hidden by bends and trees. 'I don't suppose you noticed what tyre marks there were on the track before we all started driving over it?'

'As a matter of fact we did, sir,' Conway said, not without complacency. 'We got out and checked. There were no marks except those of the Rover.'

Burns gave an approving nod, and continued to gaze around. He could see nothing on the track or beside it to indicate whether there had been any violent activity outside the car; nothing to show whether the murder had occurred here, or whether the car had been driven here with the body already in the boot. The ground itself was hard after a month of drought, and the short grass was so trampled in all directions that it looked as though a herd of elephants had passed.

'How many of these hikers were there?' he asked Conway.

'At least thirty, sir,' the sergeant told him. 'Maybe forty—they were all over the place. A club of some sort, I'd imagine.'

Burns grunted. 'Then there's not much point in bothering about footprints,' he said.

They were waiting now for the technical men to arrive. Burns was standing behind the closed boot top, staring at it in a reflective way and frowning a little.

Ryder said, 'Something worrying you, sir?'

'Just a bit, Sergeant . . . I'm puzzled by that arm.'

'You mean the way it was left sticking out?'

'Yes. It seems rather odd . . . Have you any thoughts about it?'

'Well,' Ryder said, 'I wouldn't imagine anyone would have *driven* a car with an arm sticking out like that. It would have been spotted at once, by any following car.'

'Yes. We'll be able to check the point with Carson later, I expect—but for the moment, I agree . . . So the arm got left that way when the car was already here. How, and why?'

'The murderer must have been in a hell of a hurry,' Ryder said. 'He could have opened the lid for some reason, and not noticed the arm slipping out. Or if the murder was done here, he could have bundled the body in so fast he overlooked the arm in the dark.'

'I wouldn't have thought either of those things very likely, Sergeant. Surely he'd have felt the obstruction when he lowered the lid?'

'Perhaps he just didn't care,' Ryder said.

'M'm . . . Well, that's possible . . .'

'Of course,' Ryder went on, 'we don't know for sure just how much of the arm *was* sticking out when the hikers first saw it. We can't go by what we see now—the body could have shifted when they opened the lid. If it was just a hand sticking out, the murderer might easily not have noticed it.'

Burns looked at Conway. 'Can you help on that?'

Conway shook his head. 'I'm afraid not, sir. The hikers said they saw an arm, but I suppose it could have been just a hand. I've got an address for one of them—an elderly man, name of Watson. He seemed a reliable sort of chap. He could probably tell us.'

'Good,' Burns said. 'We'll look him up.'

The specialists began to arrive soon after eleven-thirty. Carson, the county pathologist, appeared first—grumbling about his ruined Sunday morning golf but, once he was on the scene, getting down quickly to a preliminary examination of the corpse *in situ*. He was followed by Bell, the camera expert, who took close-ups and long shots of everything in sight; and by men with surveyors' tapes to record the setting of the crime in yards and feet. A mortuary vehicle and a breakdown lorry completed the muster.

For a moment or two Burns watched the pathologist. Carson's initial routine was familiar to him. Testing for rigor—the muscles of the eyelids, the lower jaw, the arms, legs and feet. Testing for temperature, with a hand under the shirt—'not quite cold,' Carson said. Looking for signs of post-mortem staining—the dark marks caused by blood draining to the lower portions of a corpse. Examining, in particular, the throat . . .

Burns said, 'When you can get the jacket off, Doc, I'd be glad if you'd take a special look at the arm that's sticking out. We can't believe the car was driven like that—but if by any chance it was, I'd expect a bruise line where the lid jolted down on the biceps. I'd like to know.'

Carson nodded briefly. 'I'll watch for it, Chief.'

While the work was going on, Burns strolled back towards the bridge, his mind occupied now with various ways in which Quarry's killer might have arrived at the track and departed from it.

The murderer could have come in the Rover—with Quarry also in it, either dead or alive. Or he could have come in a second car, and parked it somewhere close by, and walked up the track to meet a Quarry still alive. Or he could have parked farther away, on the high road, and used the overgrown path for his approach. Or—especially if he were a local man—he could have done without a car altogether and relied on his feet.

He had certainly left the immediate scene on foot, since there'd been only one set of car tracks. He could have continued to walk. Or he could have returned to the car he'd come in. Or he could have gone to a car he'd parked some time earlier in readiness for his getaway. Or he could have joined an accomplice waiting with a car near by—or been picked up by an accomplice.

These were all possibilities—and naturally there could be no answers at this stage. But at least, by the bridge, Burns found what might have been a useful facility. There was a large council lay-by, on which a huge pile of road chips had been dumped. Behind the pile a second car could have been left, or could have waited, invisible from the road. *Could* have—that was all. Because of the scattered chips, the ground showed nothing except a few spots of oil, which might well have been there for some time.

Carson was finishing his examination as Burns returned to the Rover. The superintendent watched as the body, grotesquely awkward because of the increasing rigor, was manœuvred on to a stretcher and loaded for the mortuary. With the body removed, other things became visible at the back of the boot. Burns put on his gloves again and drew out a smart leather gun-case, which proved to contain, in neat sockets, the double barrel, the stock and the various bits of equipment of a shotgun. A small silver plate on the stock bore the initials 'R.Q.' Burns held the barrels to the light and looked through them. They were smooth and gleaming. Evidently they'd been cleaned since they were last fired. He re-packed the gun and returned it to its place, noting that two boxes of cartridges in the back of the boot had not yet been opened.

The pathologist was preparing to leave, and Burns had a brief word with him. Carson's grudging and entirely provisional view was that the state of the body seemed consistent with death in the early hours of the morning—in fact, somewhere around the 2.31 shown on the clock. He would give a more considered opinion after the autopsy, which he would be doing next day. Burns promised to arrange for someone from the factory to provide the formal identification.

By now the photographers and the measurers had completed their tasks. The Rover's front wheels were lifted, and the car was towed away by the breakdown van. Burns and Ryder followed it to Lowark police station, which would be their headquarters throughout the case.

From his improvised office, Burns made his first dispositions.

Ryder was to stay at HQ, carry out a thorough examination of the Rover and its contents, supervise the fingerprinting of the bodywork—and fight off the newspapermen till the position became clearer.

Constable Williams was to contact the elderly hiker, Watson, and try to get from him the names of other hikers in the party, and bring back the evidence of at least four of them about how much of the arm had been showing when they'd first spotted it.

Burns himself would concentrate on discovering Quarry's recent movements—and the obvious first source of information was the wife. A telephone call to the police at Harpenden elicited the fact—after a brief delay for inquiries—that Mrs Alma Quarry was in residence at The Hillocks. Burns said he would break the news to her himself—but he'd be grateful if Harpenden could lend him the services of an experienced policewoman to share the burden. He would pick her up at the local station, he said, in a little over two hours.

Having arranged everything to his satisfaction for the time being, the superintendent snatched a quick sandwich and coffee in the canteen, and drove off southwards on his hundred-mile trip.

Chapter Two

Burns had visited Harpenden only once before in his life, and that was forty years ago. Then, it had been an attractive village, a small centre of tranquil life beside a common. Now, because it was no more than twenty-five miles from London, it had been drawn into the commuter belt and become a small town of little distinction and much traffic. However, the outlying country was, by residential standards, still very agreeable.

Woman Police-Constable Ellis was waiting for Burns at the station. She was a clear-eyed young woman in her late twenties and she looked dependable. It also helped that she knew the way to the Quarry home and was able to guide Burns through the somewhat featureless outer ring of the town to a quiet lane marked NO THROUGH WAY, sparsely lined with secluded and expensive dwellings. A white gate, with The Hillocks on a name plate, opened on to a hundred yards of green-tinted asphalt drive that wound among trees and bushes. The house, of salvaged mellow brick and neo-Georgian in style, stood among lawns and flowerbeds that sloped gently away to the south. The view was rural and pleasant in an unspectacular way. At the point where the drive turned in front of the house there was a well-sited cedarwood summer house, backed by trees. To the right there was a double garage, with the rear of a small Triumph car just visible through the open doors. Mrs Quarry's car, Burns assumed. Altogether, he thought, The Hillocks looked the well-kept, small country property of a very well-heeled man—which was roughly what he'd expected.

He braced himself as he rang the bell. He loathed this part of his job, as every policeman did, and years of experience had failed to inure him to it. Or even to tell him what to expect. The sudden news of death could bring collapse and prostration; tears and sobs; hysteria; petrified shock; withdrawal and silence; volubility—one never knew, for there was no common pattern of behaviour. What Burns did know, as a compassionate man, was that it was hard to be the bearer of such tidings . . .

There was a light step in the hall, and the sound of a hummed tune that broke off as the door opened. A girl stood there, smiling expectantly. A girl, at least, by Burns's standards—though she was probably in her mid-twenties. A slender brunette, whose oval face framed in a cascade of glossy black hair struck him instantly as one of the loveliest he had ever seen. An *au pair*, he wondered? A dark-eyed beauty of a daughter . . .?

He raised his bowler. 'Is Mrs Quarry at home?' he asked.

'I'm Alma Quarry,' the girl said. She looked questioningly from Burns to the uniformed policewoman, her face clouding with sudden anxiety. 'What is it?'

Burns introduced himself, and then the policewoman, trying to put off the moment of final impact. 'May we come in?' he asked.

The girl stood back to let them enter. 'Something's happened—hasn't it?' She was staring at Burns. 'Something's happened to my husband. Tell me.'

Burns said, 'I'm afraid it's bad news, Mrs Quarry. Very bad.'

'Oh, God, no . . .!'

'I'm afraid so. I'm very sorry to have to tell you that your husband is dead.'

The girl seemed held in frozen immobility. The soft lines of her face had tightened. All the beauty of a moment ago had drained away in shock and horror. Her lips moved. 'How . . .?' Her voice was a whisper. 'What happened . . .?'

'He was—attacked and killed, Mrs Quarry.'

'Oh, God,' she said again, and sagged against the wall, her hands over her face.

Burns and Policewoman Ellis between them helped her into the sitting-room, and into a chair.

There was nothing to be done, Burns knew, but wait for the first shock to pass. Certainly nothing that *he* could do. While Policewoman Ellis ministered to the girl like a nurse, quietly attending her, persuading her to take a tablet, finally making her a cup of tea, the superintendent strolled up and down the drive, patiently awaiting his moment. At some time fairly soon, if experience was anything to go by, the girl would want to talk.

He allowed some twenty minutes to pass before he re-entered the house and made his way to the sitting-room. It was empty; he could hear the murmur of voices upstairs. He glanced around, taking in the pleasant aspect of the room, the many signs of wealth and comfort. He picked up a framed photograph from a bookcase. He could just recognize the man as the Quarry he'd seen. A man approaching fifty, he guessed. In life, the face had been strong and striking. Hard-bitten, lined, determined. Two deep, vertical furrows scored the forehead. Two more deep furrows ran from the nose to the corners of the full but firm mouth. A broad, cleft chin jutted belligerently. The eyes were shrewd, calculating. A formidable, but still a handsome, face. Burns could see how its strength could have appealed to a girl . . .

There were steps in the hall, and he put the photograph down and turned. Alma Quarry came slowly in with PC Ellis and sank into a chair. Her face was drawn, her voice when she spoke was low and lifeless. But she had herself under tight control.

'Tell me what happened,' she said.

Burns told her, briefly, what he knew—the when and the where and the how of the discovery—the basic facts.

'I suppose,' she said, in the same flat voice, 'it was someone from the factory.'

'It's a possibility, certainly.'

'I've been afraid for weeks. People sent him letters. Horrible, anonymous letters . . .'

'Did he keep any of them, Mrs Quarry?'

'I don't think so—I think he destroyed them all . . . They just made him angry.' Alma stared down at the floor, her delicately arched brows drawn together in perplexity. 'I can't think what he was *doing* at Lowark last night.'

'I was going to ask you about that,' Burns said. 'We need to know his recent movements. Do you feel able to answer one or two questions?'

'I'll try . . .'

'Well, let's begin at the beginning. When did your husband leave here?'

'It was on Friday morning—about nine o'clock.'

'And what were his plans?'

'He was going to Lowark to meet the manager of the factory—John Driscoll. They were going to have lunch together and discuss the strike.'

'And then?'

'Robert was going to find a quiet hotel somewhere and rest for a night or two. He needed a rest so badly . . .'

'Because of all the trouble at the factory?'

'Yes. And this morning he was going to go shooting with John in Yorkshire—on the moors. That's where he should have been—not in Lowark. I don't understand it at all.'

'Has he been in touch with you, Mrs Quarry, since he went away?'

'Yes. I had a letter from him yesterday morning—and he telephoned, too.'

'Might I see the letter?'

'Well—yes . . .' Alma opened her handbag and took out an envelope and gave it to Burns. It had been posted, he saw, in York on the evening of Friday. The letter inside had been written on the stationery of the Moor View Hotel, Ellerbridge, Yorkshire. Under the date on the notepaper Quarry had written, 'Room 5.' The letter ran:

Dearest,

I seem to live with a telephone glued to my ear these days, so now I've got a chance to write to you I'm taking it, and enjoying the feeling of leisure it gives.

There was a pretty rowdy demonstration going on outside the factory when I got there—led by the usual militants and hooligans. Some of them started throwing things when they recognized the car, but I managed to get through without injury, thanks to the police, and I had a useful talk with John about the next steps.

Now I've settled in here for a couple of nights. You'll remember the hotel as hardly a gourmet's paradise, but I decided that in my present overstrained condition, tranquillity was more important than gastronomy. Actually, this room in the annexe is very pleasant—it's completely quiet and it has a much better outlook than the one we stayed in in the main building. I'm already feeling more relaxed—though I'm missing you very much.

John is rushing around some of the plants this weekend on urgent strike business. It's a bit complicated so I'll keep the details till I get home. Anyway, I'm very much hoping he'll be through in time for the shoot on Sunday—and I expect he will. A morning on the moors is just what we both need. Meanwhile I hope to do a bit of gentle exploring in York tomorrow, and perhaps take a look at the country around. I'll ring you tomorrow night and tell you the latest.

All my love

Robert

Burns said, Thank you, Mrs Quarry,' and gave the letter back to her. 'That was when your husband telephoned, was it—last night?'

'Yes.'

'What time would that have been?'

'I should think about a quarter to eleven.'

'Was he ringing from the hotel, do you know?'

'Yes—from his room. He said he was just turning in for an early night.'

'I see . . . Can you remember what else he said? Any details of the conversation might be helpful.'

'Well—he told me he'd spent some time on the moors in the

afternoon, driving and walking. He said he'd phoned Betty Driscoll—that's John's wife—at Lowark, and that she sent her love. The Driscolls are personal friends, you see . . . He said he'd been in touch with John at Liverpool, and John would be spending the night on his own at his cottage—he and Betty have a little weekend place near York—so they'd be able to go shooting as they'd planned, and the weather was good and he was very much looking forward to it . . . He asked me what I'd been doing and I said the Aspinalls had been in for coffee—they're neighbours of ours—and that they'd just gone . . . And that was about all . . .' Alma's voice faltered. 'Except that he said he'd be home this evening . . .'

Burns nodded gravely. 'Well, thank you, Mrs Quarry. I'm sorry I've had to trouble you about all this—but I'm sure what you've told me will be of assistance . . . Might I, by the way, have the Driscolls' address?'

'They live at Lowark,' Alma said. 'The Larches, Beaumont Lane.'

Burns made a mental note. 'Right . . . Oh, there is just one more thing—I wonder if I might have your fingerprints? We'll be going over your husband's car in the hope of finding some prints left by his assailant, and we may need yours for purposes of elimination.'

Alma gave a weary nod. 'Of course . . .'

Burns opened his bag, produced a pad and paper, invited Alma to a table, and quickly made his record. Then, like a dentist reassuringly pushing away the drill, he packed everything up and snapped the bag closed with an air of finality.

'Well, that's it . . .' He looked hard at the girl's taut face. She was still keeping a firm grip on herself—but there was bound to be a reaction soon. She'd need help and comfort when he and PC Ellis had gone—and there was no one around to give it to her. Not even a domestic.

'What are you going to do, Mrs Quarry?' he asked. 'It's not my business, of course, but I really don't think you should be here alone. Isn't there someone who could come and stay for a while? A relative, perhaps?'

Alma shook her head. 'I haven't any in this country. My relations are all in New Zealand—that's where I come from.'

'I see . . . A friend, then? I do think it's important that someone should be with you.'

'I could ask the Aspinalls, I suppose. They might come for the night . . .' She looked almost too numbed to care.

'Would you like me to speak to them?' Burns asked.

'Well—yes, if you wouldn't mind . . . I don't think I feel up to telling them . . . Their number's 304.'

Burns looked round for the telephone.

'There's one in the hall,' Alma said.

Burns went and telephoned. In a few minutes he was back. 'They'll be over right away,' he said.

There was nothing, now, to wait for. Burns said goodbye to Alma, repeating his expressions of sympathy, and regret for the intrusion, and took his departure with PC Ellis. As they were about to get into their own car, the Aspinalls' Daimler swept up the drive and stopped with a squeal of tyres. A youngish, pretty woman got out and went quickly into the house, her face full of concern. The driver, a tall, thin man with lean, sensitive features, walked over to speak to Burns.

'Was it you who telephoned just now?' he asked.

'It was,' Burns said.

'What a frightful thing, Superintendent! We're so deeply shocked, I can't tell you.'

'I understand, sir. It must seem unbelievable.'

'Absolutely! What a waste of a fine man!'

'Had you known Mr Quarry long, sir?'

'Well, not very long, as a matter of fact. They didn't come to live here till just after Christmas. But we seemed to hit it off at once. As neighbours, you know . . . What a tragedy!' Aspinall shook his head as though he were punch-drunk. 'My wife and I had been afraid something unpleasant might happen to Robert. He showed us a threatening letter he'd had. Absolutely vicious. But *murder* . . .! We certainly never thought of that. Poor Alma! We were with her only last night. She was telling us about Robert's shooting trip—she was so pleased he was having a break, and she looked so lovely, so happy . . . They've not been married a year yet, you know. It's terrible.'

Burns looked sympathetic. 'At least,' he said, 'Mrs Quarry has good friends.'

'Oh, we'll look after her—we'll do everything we can . . . But what *can* you do in such circumstances? They adored each other. It will seem like the end of the world to Alma . . . Well, goodbye, Superintendent. I'm very glad you rang us.'

'Goodbye, Mr Aspinall.'

As the front door closed behind him, the policewoman said in a low voice, 'If she adored her husband, sir, how could she take the news so calmly? She didn't shed a single tear.'

Burns paused in the act of opening the car door, 'listen!' They stood quietly. Through the open window of the sitting-room came the sound of heartbroken sobbing.

'People sometimes need a familiar shoulder to cry on,' Burns said. He eased himself in behind the wheel. 'I'll drop you at the station, Constable. You did a good job, by the way.'

Chapter Three

It had been an exhausting afternoon. Emotion, even vicarious emotion, was far more wearing than action, and Burns had been considerably affected by the young wife's tragic situation. All the same, his interest in the case was now aroused and he was anxious to press on with the investigation. Like Alma Quarry, he was wondering very much how her husband's body had come to be at Lowark when, a few hours earlier, Quarry had been about to retire for the night near York, a hundred-odd miles away. The place to start asking was obviously the hotel. The MI motorway, running close by Harpenden, would take him there in a little over three hours; the trail should still be warm when he arrived. He set down PC Ellis at her headquarters, with a final word of thanks, and was soon driving north at a steady seventy. He stopped only once, for petrol and a brief snack at a service station, and by seven-thirty in the evening he had reached the Moor View Hotel.

Moor View was a two-star country house hotel, hidden away in a network of lanes some twelve miles north of York. It had, as Burns was soon to discover, both the merits and the demerits of its type. It was agreeably situated in extensive grounds and, except for the humming of a generator, was very quiet. Its public rooms had space and dignity; it housed some fine old furniture and pictures, and its atmosphere was pleasantly informal. But it was also dingy, down-at-heel and draughty; serviced by a willing but ill-trained staff drawn mainly from the local village; and managed by a thin, tense woman who looked as though the burden of hotel-keeping was becoming too much for her—the former daughter of the house and now its genteel owner, Lady Pamela Everton.

Lady Pamela, it appeared, had heard the news of Robert Quarry's murder on the radio at six o'clock. She was still visibly shaken, and nervously anxious to tell all she knew once the superintendent had identified himself.

'Well, let's start at the beginning,' Burns said, as he settled into a chair in her private parlour. 'When did Mr Quarry arrive here?'

'Just after tea-time on Friday evening,' Lady Pamela told him.

'Had he made a reservation?'

'No—he just dropped in.'

'What did he say?'

'He said he'd like to stay with us for two nights, and that he was looking forward to a restful weekend. We talked about the rooms, and he finally settled on one in the annexe, because he liked the view.'

Burns nodded. 'What was the arrangement—full board?'

'No—just dinner, bed and breakfast. He expected to be out for lunch each day.'

'I see. Now have you any idea how he occupied himself while he was here? I'd be glad to hear anything you can tell me about his movements—starting from the time he arrived.'

'Well, let me think . . . He didn't have tea that first day—I remember noticing him going off in his car soon after he'd arranged about his room.'

'I imagine he drove into York,' Burns said. 'His wife received a letter from him there. Was he back in time for dinner?'

'Oh, yes. And after dinner he watched television . . . Yesterday he was out in his car all day. I had a chat with him in the evening and he told me he'd spent the morning in York—he was very enthusiastic about the Minster and the old houses inside the wall, which he hadn't seen before . . . And in the afternoon he'd been up on the moors, he said . . . Well, then he had dinner, and soon afterwards he went off to his room. That's really all I can tell you.'

'When, in fact, was he last seen?'

'It was a little after half-past ten last night. He telephoned from his room for a large whisky-and-soda, and Ames, the porter, took it to him. He was in bed, reading ... It seems quite unbelievable that he could have been found murdered in Lowark this morning.'

'It's certainly very puzzling,' Burns agreed. 'When was he missed, Lady Pamela?'

'Just before nine o'clock to-day. A friend of his—a Mr Driscoll—arrived at the hotel at about ten to nine. Apparently he and Mr Quarry had arranged to have breakfast together here before going off for a morning's shooting. Mr Driscoll had called at Mr Quarry's room on his way in, and got no reply to his knock, and he'd looked around the hotel and in the grounds, and then he'd discovered that Mr Quarry's car had gone. He asked if any message had been left for him, but none had, and of course he was very surprised.'

'I can imagine ... So what did you do?'

'Well,' Lady Pamela said, with some embarrassment, 'I thought I'd better look in Mr Quarry's room. I couldn't believe he'd gone off without paying—particularly as he'd stayed here once before with his wife, and I'd found them a charming couple—but strange things do happen in the hotel business. So I went across with Mr Driscoll to see.'

'What did you find?'

'Very much what I expected. The bed had been slept in, and the lights were all turned off. Mr Quarry's suitcase was on the stand, and some of his clothes were in the wardrobe, and his night things were on the bed. It was obvious that he'd simply got up early and gone out. At least, that's what I thought.'

'Understandably,' Burns said. 'So then what happened?'

'Well, I asked Mr Driscoll if he was sure he hadn't made a mistake about his arrangement with Mr Quarry. I thought there could have been some confusion about the date or the time. But he was certain there hadn't been—and he was rather disturbed.'

'What did he do?'

'He had breakfast here, hoping that Mr Quarry would return, and when there was still no sign of him at ten o'clock he went off for an hour or two. He came back about midday and asked if there was any news, but of course there wasn't. Then he said he was going home to Lowark, and that he'd leave a message for Mr Quarry. At three o'clock this afternoon he telephoned me from Lowark, but I still couldn't give him any news, of course?'

'Have you got the note he left?'

'Yes, it's here.' Lady Pamela went to a bureau and produced a sealed envelope addressed to 'Robert Quarry, Esq.' Burns opened it. The message read: 'Something's obviously happened, but I can't imagine what. I'm going back to Lowark. Give me a ring when you surface. John.'

Burns passed the note to Lady Pamela, who read it.

'Did you think of taking any steps yourself?' he asked, 'about your missing guest?'

'No, I didn't,' Lady Pamela said. 'From my point of view, as a hotel-keeper, there was no reason for concern. A guest had gone off early in the morning, as I thought, and everything suggested he was going to return. It hardly seemed my business, what he was doing. Of course, if I'd had any idea . . .'

'Quite so.' Burns was silent for a moment. 'I believe Mr Quarry made some telephone calls while he was here?'

'Yes, he did.'

'Have you any record of them?'

'We know the numbers,' Lady Pamela said, 'because he phoned from his room and we had to get them for him. And we know the cost, of course . . .' She extracted a slip of paper from a file in the bureau. 'One was to a Lowark number, late yesterday afternoon. That was Lowark 31400. It was just after Mr Quarry had come in. Then, very soon afterwards, he made a call to Liverpool—05273. And last night, at about a quarter to eleven, he spoke to a number at Harpenden. That was 032.'

The calls, subject to check, were in accordance with what Burns had already been told. The Lowark one would have been to Betty Driscoll, the Liverpool one to Driscoll, the Harpenden one to Alma Quarry. He made a note of the numbers. 'No others, Lady Pamela?'

'No others through our switchboard. There's a public box in the lobby—he might have used that, of course.'

'True . . . Were there any incoming calls for him while he was here, do you know?'

'Not that I'm aware of. But I'll make sure and let you know.'

'Thank you . . . Did he leave any message for anyone at any time, or receive any message from anyone?'

'No.'

'Did he have any letters or visitors?'

'No.'

Burns grunted. 'Tell me, Lady Pamela, how did he strike you while he was here? Did he seem worried, preoccupied, bad-tempered, off his food—anything like that?'

Lady Pamela shook her head. 'Nothing like that at all, Superintendent. He just seemed to be enjoying his restful weekend. He was relaxed and cheerful and friendly. In fact, the perfect guest.'

'M'm . . .' Burns sat pondering for a moment. Then he rose. 'Well, perhaps I might take a look at his room?'

The Moor View's annexe proved to be a long, single-storied building of quite pleasing lines, situated about fifty yards below the main block of the hotel. It had nine bedrooms, each with a bathroom *en suite*. Access to the rooms was by a single corridor. Lady Pamela unlocked the door of number 5 with her master key, switched on the light and showed Burns in.

The superintendent gave an inward sigh as he gazed around. The room, he saw, had been 'done.' The bed had been re-made. Quarry's pyjamas had been folded and tucked under a pillow. His dressing-gown had been hung up in the bathroom. No whisky glass or soda syphon was to be seen. Everything had been tidied up . . . Not that Burns could blame anyone, exasperating though it was. No one could have supposed, that morning, that Quarry had been murdered.

The suitcase on the stand wasn't locked, and he sifted through the few contents that had been left in it. There were a couple of shirts, a change of underclothes, socks and handkerchiefs, a half-full box of cigars, and various oddments—nothing of any interest. He moved on, noting the plus-fours and shooting-jacket hanging in the wardrobe, and glancing at the paperback spy thriller lying by the bedside lamp. He crossed to the window. It was a low, casement window, hooked open about six inches. The cheap cotton curtains were billowing a little in the night breeze.

'Was this window open when you came in this morning?' he asked.

Lady Pamela nodded. 'Just like that. It was a very mild night.'

'How were the curtains?'

'They were half drawn. Enough to let the light in.'

'I see.' Burns opened the window wide, produced a small torch from his pocket, and flashed it around outside. There was a narrow tarmac path running the length of the block beneath the windows. Beyond the path he could see the outline of shrubs against the sky.

'I assume this path goes round the budding and joins the drive,' he said.

'That's right, Superintendent.'

'Which of the other annexe rooms were occupied last night?'

'Only number 9—that's the one at the end, nearest the house. We only have a few guests at this time of year, and most of them prefer the main building.'

Burns nodded. 'Then it won't inconvenience you, will it, if I ask you to keep this room shut up for a day or so? I'm afraid I've arrived rather late on the scene—but I'd still like to have it thoroughly examined before it's used again.'

'Very well, Superintendent. 'I'll give instructions that no one is to come in.'

'Thank you.' Burns studied the window ledge for a moment, then closed the casement. 'If I may,' he said, 'I'd like to stay over for the night. In a room next door, perhaps?'

'By all means. I'll put you in number 4.'

'Am I too late for a meal?'

'Well, it's past our normal dinner-time, of course,' Lady Pamela said. 'But in the special circumstances I'm sure we can provide something.'

Even when all allowances were made for the fact that the food had been warmed up, it seemed to Burns to be quite awful. The soup was watery, the wedge of fish tasteless, the steak pie unaccountably flavoured with some cheap cooking oil that gave him instant indigestion. If *he* had been choosing a hotel, he reflected, he would have put gastronomy before tranquillity—especially if, like Quarry, he had known the form. Or better still, he'd have looked for some place that reasonably combined both features. There was certainly no accounting for tastes . . .

With dinner an unfortunately recurring memory, he retired to his room to do some telephoning. First he rang Alice to say he wouldn't be home—which in no way surprised her. Once he was out on a case it often happened that he had to spend the night away. Then he called up Sergeant Ryder at his house, which in no way surprised the sergeant. Burns gave him a concise but comprehensive account of his discoveries at the Quarry home and at the hotel, and asked for a fingerprint and photo unit to be sent to the Moor View first thing in the morning.

'Tell them I want everything in the room checked, Sergeant—particularly the area round the window.'

'Very good, sir, I'll arrange it,' Ryder said, his cheerfulness not diminished by the lateness of the hour.

'Will you also get on to John Driscoll at Lowark 31400 and tell him I'll be calling on him at his home at eleven-thirty tomorrow morning? If he was a friend of Quarry's he'll probably be feeling upset—and I've had all the emotion I can take for one day.'

'I'll attend to it, sir.'

'Good. Now, what's the position at your end?'

'Well, we got the car fingerprinted, and the report's in. The steering-wheel was mostly smudged. There were only two clear prints on it—both Quarry's.'

'M'm . . . Whereabouts were they?'

'Near the top of the wheel—about as high as anyone would hold it. One on each side. Left thumb and right first finger.'

'I see . . . What else?'

'Various prints on the coachwork—some Quarry's, others not identified. No prints at all where "Bastard" was written. That could have been done with a gloved fingertip, of course. Probably was, or there'd be something where the writing stopped. Quarry's prints are all over the gun—no one else's. That's the lot for the moment.'

'How about the contents of the car? Did you come across anything interesting?'

'Nothing sensational, sir. The usual collection of oddments. A few missiles.'

'Missiles!'

'Well, that's my guess. A lump of putty, a small pebble, and about a dozen loose pennies.'

'Ah!—the factory, I suppose. He didn't get his window up soon enough.'

'That's about it . . . There is one more thing I ought to mention, sir. It seems Quarry had his car serviced yesterday by a York garage—Fleetway Cars. I found a counterfoil in the service book, stamped and dated by the garage, with the mileage at the time of the service written in. The thing is, there's a discrepancy.'

'Oh? What?'

'Well, the mileage recorded by the garage is 36,501, but the speedometer registers only 36,459—forty-two miles less. And of course the car's done quite a trip since the service—from the garage to the hotel, and from the hotel to Lowark—apart from any running around.'

Burns grunted. 'It sounds as though someone at the garage didn't take the reading properly.'

'I should think that's it, sir.'

'Still, we ought to make sure.' Burns reflected. 'You'd better drive up in the morning, Sergeant—you've got the service book and they'll need to see it. I'll talk to Driscoll, and we'll meet at HQ tomorrow afternoon. Okay?'

'Very good, sir,' Ryder said.

Before he retired for the night, Burns conducted a small experiment. He opened his casement window wide and climbed out on to the path. The sill was so low that, even for a man of his build, there was no difficulty—it involved little more than putting a leg over.

Outside, he stood listening. Lights in the main block showed that people were still up—but he could hear no sound from them. He looked along the path. There was a glow from the window of room 9 at the end of the annexe. He walked quietly along to it. Through a gap in the curtains he could see the white thatch of an old man's head above a chair-back, and the top of a newspaper. The old man made no move—evidently he'd heard nothing. Burns returned to his window, climbed back in, and went to bed.

The night proved as tranquil as he'd been led to expect. Not a murmur of sound disturbed his solid sleep. He woke early, to a bright clear day, feeling younger than his years. Now, for the first time, he was able to see the view from the annexe window—and it was undoubtedly rewarding. There was a long descending vista of russet-tinted trees, framed by the gaps in the shrubbery, and in the far distance the rounded tops of purple moors. He could well appreciate how a man of Quarry's sporting tastes would have gone for such a view. In much the same way, Burns himself might have chosen some hotel room that overlooked a trout stream or a lake.

Breakfast at the Moor View, even on weekdays, didn't begin until eight-thirty, and Burns filled in the time with an exploratory tour of the grounds. First he went round to the shrubbery to see if he could find any trace of footmarks between the bushes—but the earth was hard and dry, and nothing showed. Nor was there anything to mark his own excursion along the tarmac path the night before. He walked round the block to the drive and looked towards the entrance gate. The hotel grounds, he saw, sloped quite steeply to the lane a hundred yards below—and the lane itself also sloped away. There was, it appeared, no formal car-park. Guests' cars were parked along the drive wherever there was room—and with the hotel sparsely occupied, there was plenty of room. Burns asked the porter, Ames, if he knew where Mr Quarry had parked his car—and Ames indicated a spot some twenty yards below the annexe.

The breakfast gong had still not sounded, and Burns took the opportunity to glance at the newspapers he'd ordered. As he'd expected, the Quarry murder was featured prominently in all. There were photographs of the dead man, accounts of his career and achievements, and much speculation about the relevance of the Lowark strike to the murder. There were pictures of the track, with the murder spot marked X, and several imaginative reconstructions of what might have happened. There were also one or two pictures of Burns himself, under captions like 'Man in Charge', and 'Last Case', with references to his coming retirement. Ryder, Burns guessed, had done a little talking—but not about anything that mattered.

After breakfast Burns had another short session with Lady Pamela, going over the list of guests. There had been twelve on Saturday night, apart from Quarry, and all were still in residence. They were made up of four elderly couples, two retired schoolmistresses, the old gentleman in number 9, and a single girl who was on a sketching trip. Before he left, Burns questioned each of them. What time had they gone to bed on Saturday? Had they heard or seen anything unusual in the grounds? In particular, had they heard any car on the move, and if so when? The answers were all negative. It seemed that everyone at the Moor View had been snugly tucked up by eleven o'clock on Saturday night, and no one had heard a thing.

After which conscientious bit of routine, Burns set off for Lowark.

Chapter Four

The Driscolls' home proved to be almost as affluent-looking as The Hillocks—but in a less suburban way. It was a long, low house of creeper-clad brick, probably a hundred years old, set in well-tended and secluded grounds a mile or two outside Lowark. A walled garden descended in a staircase of shaved lawns to a frontage on the river Trent, where a smart little cabin boat was moored. Two cars were parked outside the garage—a big Jaguar and a sporty red MG.

As Burns cut his engine, Driscoll emerged from the house and crossed the drive to meet him. He was a gaunt and gangling man, very tall, with a bony face and a look of gristly energy. In age he appeared roughly the contemporary of Quarry. He greeted Burns with grave courtesy and conducted him into the sitting-room, where his wife was waiting. Betty Driscoll was a handsome blonde of perhaps thirty-five, blue-eyed and shapely. It wasn't quite a case of Beauty and the Beast, but the phrase did edge into Burns' mind. The women in this case, he reflected, seemed to be outstandingly attractive; the men, somewhat otherwise. But that, he realized, was a man's view.

Superficially, at least, there was no mistaking the sense of shock that still pervaded the Driscoll home. The couple, standing together, had the sad air of mourners at a graveside. Burns offered his condolences on the tragedy. Betty Driscoll said she could still hardly believe it had happened. Burns said he hoped the appointment he'd made hadn't been too inconvenient. Driscoll said the lost morning was no sacrifice if it would help in the apprehension of the murderer.

Burns put his bowler on a chair, and Betty suggested they should sit down.

When they were seated, Burns said, 'What I need at this stage is information—as much as I can get. I saw Mrs Quarry yesterday, and she was helpful, but naturally she wasn't in a state to do much talking. I've just come from the Moor View Hotel, where I picked up a few more facts, but I hardly know enough yet to ask intelligent questions. So what I would like, Mr Driscoll, is that you should tell me everything you can—about the arrangements you made with Mr Quarry for the weekend, about the background situation, about Quarry himself—anything you consider relevant to what's happened.'

'Very well . . .' There was a short pause as Driscoll ordered his thoughts. 'I think I'd better start with the strike at the factory, because it's that that led up to everything and that everything turns on . . . You know about the strike, of course?'

'I know something about it,' Burns said. 'I'd be glad to hear more.'

'Well, it's been going on for weeks, now, and it's an unmitigated disaster for everyone concerned. It's costing us a fantastic sum in lost production and it's put thousands of people out of work—not just our own people, but workers in several car plants that rely on our components. It began, as you probably know, over the dismissal of a shop steward named Tom Sullivan—a real troublemaker, who's gained a lot of influence over the men. Very eloquent chap.'

Burns nodded. 'I've read about him.'

'Sullivan deliberately flouted the company rules. It got to the point where he was virtually taking over the plant premises for militant plotting in working time. So we sacked him. And Robert Quarry, as chairman of the group, made it plain that we'd never employ him in Lowark again . . . Well, right from the beginning, the mood of a section of the men was very ugly. Robert and I both had anonymous letters threatening us with violence. Sullivan openly boasted at one factory-gate meeting that he was going to "get Quarry"—or so it was reported to me. There've been repeated demonstrations, and several near-riots. The struggle became even more bitter the week before last, when Robert issued an ultimatum. He said if the men weren't back within fourteen days he'd close the Lowark factory for good and switch its production to Bristol. Since when we've been deadlocked . . . I hope this doesn't all seem too remote to you, Superintendent.'

'On the contrary,' Burns said, 'it's exactly what I wanted to hear.' He was impressed by Driscoll's lucid and incisive manner. The man's angular appearance seemed matched by a no less rugged intelligence.

'Well,' Driscoll went on, 'a few days ago a tiny chink of light opened. The *Lowark Advertiser*, our weekly paper, published a joint letter from a number of prominent local citizens suggesting that the dispute might be resolved without loss of face by either side if Sullivan could be transferred to another of the group's factories—in Bristol or Liverpool—where as a newcomer he would have no authority or influence. It was an impressive letter—perhaps you'd like to see it.' He glanced at his wife. 'Would you get it, darling? It's on my desk.' Betty went out, and returned almost at once with a marked copy of the newspaper, which she gave to Burns. Driscoll said, 'Take it with you, Superintendent—I've got others.' Burns nodded, and slipped the paper into his bag. Driscoll resumed. 'Anyhow, *I* thought the idea had possibilities, so on Wednesday—the day the paper came out—I posted a copy to Robert. He phoned me on Thursday and said he'd like to discuss the matter, and he suggested driving up on Friday and joining me for a working lunch.'

'Was that when he also suggested you might go shooting on Sunday?'

'That's right. We'd shot together several times before. I rent a stretch of moor on the fringe of the York national park, and we both enjoyed a pot at the birds. So I said, fine, we'd do that.'

'And he joined you on Friday as arranged.'

'Yes—he turned up at the factory just before twelve. There was a noisy mob outside, picketing and demonstrating, with Sullivan very much in evidence, and Robert had to have police help to get through after his car had been pretty thoroughly pelted. It would have been wiser, I suppose, to have chosen a quieter rendezvous, but that wasn't Robert's way—he always preferred to meet trouble head-on. Anyhow, we fought our way out again, and lunched in town, and discussed the proposition. I think I was more in favour of exploring the possibilities than Robert, but he wasn't totally opposed. He'd been under tremendous pressure for a settlement, of course, from all sorts of quarters—some of them pretty powerful. In the end he suggested that I should visit Bristol and Liverpool right away, talk the thing over with the managers there, and get their views. He would drive north, rest up in some hotel for a couple of nights, and get in touch with me again on Saturday after checking with my wife where I was. We'd then make final arrangements about the Sunday shoot.'

'Let me get this clear,' Burns said. 'You couldn't arrange to communicate with him directly because at that time you didn't know where he was going to stay. And he couldn't communicate with you directly because you were on the move between cities. So your wife was to act as a sort of telephone exchange.'

'Exactly.'

'Good . . . Go on, Mr Driscoll.'

'Well, everything worked out very smoothly. I rang my wife from Liverpool on Saturday and told her I'd be at the Adelphi Hotel there until six o'clock. Robert rang her soon afterwards, as we'd planned, and she told him where I was and gave him my phone number. Then Robert rang me, and we fixed everything.'

'What, exactly, was the final arrangement?'

'I told him I proposed to spend Saturday night at the cottage my wife and I have in Yorkshire—there seemed no point in driving all the way to Lowark and back again. Robert said in that case how about meeting him at his hotel for breakfast—which seemed a good idea, since it was on the way to the moor where we were going to shoot. He told me he was staying in the hotel annexe, and he gave me his room number. "Just bang on my door when you get here," he said. "I'll be ready, and we'll go in to breakfast together." I told him I'd be there sharp at nine. We had a brief word about my trip—we didn't go into details, as we knew we'd have the whole of Sunday morning to discuss it . . . And that was that.'

'What, in fact, *was* the result of your trip, Mr Driscoll?'

'It was better than I'd expected. The Bristol manager thought that if Sullivan could be persuaded, or bribed, to make the move, he could be absorbed without too much difficulty. Liverpool wasn't so sure—they're a wild lot, there. The thing is, at Bristol the union officials have a strong grip on the situation, and so far they've managed to keep the militants under control.'

'I see . . . Well, let's get back to your own movements. You spent the night alone at your cottage. I take it you thought that preferable to putting up at a hotel for the night.'

'It didn't occur to me to do anything else, Superintendent. If you've got a *pied-à-terre*, why pay for a hotel? We leave the heaters on at this time of year, and there's always something to eat in the fridge. It was the obvious place to stop.'

'I understand. And, having spent the night there, you turned up at the Moor View at nine to keep the appointment?'

'Yes—in good spirits and with a healthy appetite . . . No doubt they told you at the hotel what happened then.'

'I gathered you tried Quarry's room, searched around for him, discovered his car had gone, and asked if there was any message.'

'That's right.'

'And the state of his room, when you saw it, suggested that he'd dressed and gone out early.'

'Yes.'

'What did you make of it, Mr Driscoll? What did you think?'

'Well, at first I was quite baffled. Robert had always been a most reliable person—it wasn't in the least like him to mess up an engagement. Then, when I began to think it over, I could see possible explanations. I knew he was an early riser and a very active man, and I thought perhaps he'd taken advantage of the fine morning to drive up to the moors before breakfast—and that his car had broken down. I imagined him trudging back for help, perhaps miles. I also thought of the possibility of illness—or accident.'

'You didn't feel you should do anything about it—like ringing the police, or Mrs Quarry?'

'I considered it,' Driscoll said, 'but at first I decided against it. I didn't want to alarm Alma unnecessarily, and I certainly didn't want to start any kind of police hue and cry if there was no need. Robert was a close friend of mine, but he was also my boss, and he wouldn't have taken kindly to a lot of fuss if there hadn't been anything wrong. I had breakfast, and waited for a bit, and then I went off to the cottage, and tidied the place up, and left my gun. Around lunchtime I called back at the hotel, and scribbled a note, and then I came home and discussed the whole situation with my wife.'

'By then, you must have been very worried.'

'Yes, we were—in fact we'd practically decided we'd have to inform the police. Then, about four o'clock, a reporter from the *Lowark Advertiser* rang up and told us the news. We were absolutely shattered. My wife rang Alma at once, of course—she was all set to go straight down to Harpenden—but a neighbour answered the phone and said Alma had taken some pills and was asleep, and that everything was under control . . .' Driscoll drew a long breath. 'It was a truly dreadful day, Superintendent—I can tell you that.'

'So I can imagine,' Burns said. He was silent for a moment. 'Well, you've given me a very full and detailed account of everything that happened as far as you're concerned, Mr Driscoll—and I'm grateful. Would you care, now, to tell me more about Quarry as a man? Obviously you knew him pretty well.'

Driscoll nodded. 'I knew him *very* well, Superintendent—we were old friends. We were in the REs together in 1944—two very young men, then—and we landed on the same beach on D-day. I was scared as hell, but Robert was a really tough fighter—he'd done some Commando jobs earlier in the war and he'd actually enjoyed them. He distinguished himself over and over again—he just couldn't help it—and he finished the war with a chestful of gongs. When he was demobbed he went into industry—*threw* himself into it, you might say—and he never looked back. He wasn't just a first-rate technician—he was an organizer and leader as well. We kept in touch, and after a while he took me into the company he'd built up, and pushed me along—probably for old times' sake. Not that I haven't done a good job; I think I have—but I certainly owe him a tremendous debt.'

'You admired him a great deal?'

'I certainly admired him for *some* things,' Driscoll said. 'Not for all . . . He was an outstanding man, there's no doubt about that. A very forceful, very impressive man. I admired his courage and his drive and his determination. His loyalty, too. As long as you had his trust he'd never let you down—you could rely on him absolutely. But . . .' Driscoll hesitated. 'How shall I put it? Sometimes I felt he was too full of rectitude. He was certainly intolerant. He had strong views and strong feelings, and he always assumed he was right . . . And he lacked compassion. He was a stern, unbending man, who saw everything in black and white. By my standards, his sense of justice was a bit primitive. You know—an eye for an eye, that sort of thing . . .'

'It doesn't sound to me as though he was a particularly amiable character,' Burns said.

'Well, he was two-sided—that's what I'm really trying to say. He was amiable enough with people he was fond of. He was very attentive to Alma, and he was always very decent to me. The thing is, he was a most positive personality; larger than life in whatever he did. If he felt generous he could be magnificently generous. If he liked you, he could be an incomparable friend; if he disliked you he could be terrifying. I suppose the truth is he had a touch of—what do they call it?—*folie de grandeur*. Just a touch . . . All the same, he had great qualities and you had to respect him.'

Burns looked at Betty, who until now had sat silent, watching her husband and following his words with close attention. 'And you, Mrs Driscoll—would you agree with your husband's analysis?'

'I think it's probably fair,' she said slowly, 'though I'm not as competent to judge as he is. I didn't know Robert all that well. I'd met him many times, of course—when he came to lunch here to talk business with John, and when he and Alma were guests at our cottage, and sometimes when we all met socially in London or Harpenden . . . But I wouldn't say I ever *knew* him . . . He certainly gave me the impression of being rather ruthless, and there were moments when I felt I couldn't stand him. But he was a most interesting and fascinating man, all the same. I'm very very sorry we shan't see him again.'

Burns gave a sympathetic nod, and turned once more to Driscoll. 'From what you said earlier—about the strike leading up to everything—I gather you've pretty definite views about the murder. What's your theory?'

'The obvious one,' Driscoll said. 'I haven't the slightest doubt that the killing arose out of the factory situation. Violence has been in the air for weeks—violence and hatred. We all shared the responsibility for the decisions that were taken—but Robert was made the target. If I were asked to guess, I'd guess that one or more strikers followed him from Lowark on Friday, snatched him from his room on Saturday night and brought him back here to kill him.'

'Just out of malice?'

'Perhaps not *just* malice. There could have been a practical reason, too.'

'What reason?'

'Well—who knows what will happen now about the strike? Robert might have modified his position a little, under pressure, but he'd never have given in. And he wouldn't have allowed the Board to give in. Effectively, he *was* the Board while he was alive. Now that he's gone, it wouldn't surprise me if they opted for unconditional surrender.'

'Are you suggesting that that might have been the motive for the murder? To get rid of the obstacle to a settlement—to end the strike?'

'It's in my mind, Superintendent.'

'M'm . . . The same motive, of course, could have applied not just to a striker, but to anyone else who was being harmed by the strike. Even—to take an extreme example—a fellow industrialist who was losing money because of it.'

'That's theoretically possible, I suppose—but it's a pretty

far-fetched notion. We all know it's the militant lefties who go for violence, organize the demos, make the petrol bombs. *I* think the murderer came from the factory.'

'Have you anyone specifically in mind for the role?'

Driscoll shrugged. 'Sullivan sticks out, doesn't he? I know he's a talker, a big mouth—it's quite possible he wouldn't have had the guts for a killing. But I'd be interested to hear what he was doing on Saturday night, all the same.'

'Do you know his address?'

'I do, indeed—there's been quite a correspondence with him since the sacking. It's number 12, Wilson Street.'

Burns made a note. 'Well,' he said, getting up, 'that would seem to be as far as we can go at the moment. Thank you both very much for your help. No doubt we shall be in touch again.' He gave Betty Driscoll an old-fashioned bow, and shook hands with Driscoll, at the same time scrutinizing him carefully. As far as he could see, the manager showed no signs of any injury.

Chapter Five

At about the time that Burns was interviewing the Driscolls in Lowark, Sergeant Ryder was turning into the garage of Fleetway Cars in York. It was a large and active establishment, with a forecourt lined with secondhand cars, a showroom, and a big repairs unit. Ryder sought out the manager in his office, and identified himself. 'I'm looking into the murder of Robert Quarry,' he said, unfolding the newspaper he was carrying. It was a copy of the *Mail* of that morning, and much of its front page was taken up with the murder.

'Quarry . . .?' The manager glanced at the headlines. 'Oh, the Lowark man. Yes, I read about it. A pretty nasty business, I thought.' He looked a bit puzzled. 'Why come to me, Sergeant?'

'I believe your garage serviced his car on Saturday.'

The manager glanced at Ryder in astonishment. 'Serviced his car!' He took the newspaper and studied a rather blotchy photograph of Quarry.

Slowly, his expression changed. 'You know,' he said, 'I think you're right. It's not much of a likeness, but I do remember him now. He had a Rover . . .'

'Yes—a beige 3-litre.'

'Correct. So that was Quarry? Well, I'm damned!'

'He didn't give a name, I take it.'

'No—it was just a casual job. There wasn't any need.'

'What time did he bring the car in?' Ryder asked.

'Oh, quite early—it must have been soon after nine. He said the service was a bit overdue and he was finding the steering stiff, and could we oblige him. We weren't too busy, so I said okay. The car was ready for him when he got back at twelve, and he paid cash and took it away. It was a routine job, no problems.'

'Well, there's a little problem now,' Ryder said. He produced the service book and explained what he'd come about.

The manager looked at the book. Then he went to his office door and shouted to the workshop foreman. 'Bill, who serviced that 3-litre Rover on Saturday?' A shout came back. 'Jock and Terry.' 'Is Jock there?' 'No, he's delivering the new Jag.' 'Is Terry around?' 'Yes, he's here.' 'Tell him I'd like to see him, will you?' 'Okay.'

In a few moments, Terry appeared. He was a pleasant-faced youth in his late teens.

The manager said, 'That Rover service you helped with on Saturday . . . Did Jock record the mileage, or did you?' He showed the youth the figure written in on the counterfoil—36,501.

'I did.'

'Did you take the reading yourself?'

'Yes, sir.'

Ryder said, in a friendly tone, 'Could you say for certain, Terry, that you got the figure right?'

Terry hesitated. 'I dunno about *certain*. I thought I did.'

'Did you get inside the car to take it—or did you just look in from the outside?'

Terry considered. 'I guess I just looked in.'

'I see. I was wondering—do you suppose you could have mistaken a 3 for a 5? Could the figure have been 36,301?'

'I suppose it could,' Terry admitted. 'They're a bit alike.'

Ryder nodded. 'Okay, young feller. Don't worry—there's no harm done. I only wanted to check.'

Terry glanced at the manager, got a nod of dismissal, and slipped away.

The manager said, with a tolerant smile, 'He meets his girl for lunch most Saturdays—I'll bet he was in a hurry to get away.' He walked out with Ryder to the forecourt. 'Well, I hope you catch the killer, Sergeant. A strike's one thing, murder's another. I don't know what this country's coming to . . .'

Chapter Six

Whatever hardships Tom Sullivan might have been suffering as a result of his six weeks' absence from work without strike pay, none was immediately apparent to Burns when he called at number 12, Wilson Street, one of a row of newish council houses, shortly after lunch. A small boy below school age was cavorting about the lawn on an expensive tricycle. In the porch, a baby was crying intermittently in an expensive pram. Through the front window Burns caught the flicker of a colour TV set. Sullivan himself was washing down a smart blue Vauxhall Viva in the road outside the gate. Social security and HP appeared to be taking care of his essential needs.

Burns said, 'Good afternoon, Mr Sullivan. I'm Detective Chief Superintendent Burns, and I'm investigating the murder of Robert Quarry. I'd like a word with you.'

Sullivan said 'Yeah?', and went on washing the saloon. He was a small, narrow-chested man with a bulbous forehead, beetling eyebrows and a tiny mouth down-turned at the corners. A frayed pullover, dirty open-necked shirt and down-at-heel shoes gave him a slovenly appearance, but by odd contrast he seemed to have had a carefully-styled hair-do, so that locks of hair were draped over and around his head in unlikely positions. He showed no sign of wishing to add to his monosyllable.

Burns strolled round the car, cocking an eye at the windscreen. There was one economy, he saw, that Sullivan had made.

'I suppose you know,' he said, 'that your road fund licence expired three weeks ago?'

Sullivan grunted. 'What's three weeks? Anyway, I'm not driving the car.'

'It's out on the highway, unlicensed. That's an offence.'

'All right, I'll see to it . . . I'm a bit short of cash.'

'You'll be shorter still if I book you,' Burns said amiably. 'Come on, Sullivan, how about a little co-operation?'

Sullivan looked at him across the top of the car. 'What's on your mind, then?'

'I'm told,' Burns said, 'that you were heard to threaten Quarry. That you said in public you were going to "get him".'

Sullivan shrugged. 'So what? That didn't mean anything physical. It just meant I was going to beat him in the strike.'

'Murder would have been one way of doing it.'

'Well, it wouldn't have been my way. Not that I'm shedding any tears over the sod—he had it coming to him. He was a real bastard.'

'That's what the murderer wrote on his car.'

'So I read in the paper. But *I* didn't have anything to do with it.'

'Perhaps you've some idea who did?'

'Course I haven't. You're wasting your time coming to see me, mate. Just because I've spoken up for three thousand workers in a legitimate way to make sure they don't get beaten into the ground by a rich capitalist bastard, it doesn't mean I was mixed up in a murder. I s'pose you're trying to pin something on me so you can shut me up and stop the strike. I know you lot—I know you're always in cahoots with the bosses. Well, you're on a loser this time, I can tell you. The workers of Lowark'll go on standing up for their rights and they'll win, because it's the lads on the shop floor that are the bosses now, not those smart bastards who think they're running the show in London, and the sooner they realize that times have changed and that we do the work and we're going to call the tune . . .' Sullivan stopped washing and waved a clenched fist—a political gesture somewhat marred by the fact that it held a chamois leather. 'You can take it from me the lads in this town are absolutely solid and they'll stay out till they get their way and soon they'll get others to join them and the workers'll all march together . . .'

'Save your breath, Sullivan,' Burns said shortly. 'I'm not a public meeting. Just tell me what you were doing on Saturday night, will you?'

Sullivan, checked in mid-flight, gazed sulkily at the superintendent. 'I was looking at the telly. With the missus and three of the kids.'

'Till when?'

'Till about midnight.'

'And then?'

'Then we all went to bed. Okay with you?'

'We'll see,' Burns said. He moved closer and scrutinized the little man. He could see no signs of any injuries. In any case, he couldn't imagine Sullivan lasting long in a fight with his late boss. Not, at least, in a fair fight. Not without help . . .

He had no alibi, of course. Nothing you could call an alibi. But that attitude of truculent contempt didn't normally go with guilt. He had a car he could have used—but what man in his senses would set out on a murderous journey in a car with an out-of-date licence? On the whole, Burns was inclined to think that his visit *had* been a waste of time.

Chapter Seven

A bunch of newspapermen and a TV crew were waiting outside headquarters when Burns got back in the late afternoon. One of the local men recognized him, notebooks came out hopefully, cameras started clicking, and up on the TV van there was a brief burst of filming.

Burns paused for a second. 'I'm afraid I've nothing to tell you at this stage, gentlemen. The investigation has only just begun. We have no lead so far, and there are no suspects. Try again in a few days' time.' He listened with an urbane smile to a couple of questions, shook his head, and continued into his office. Ryder was alone there, studying some figures he'd jotted down on a pad.

Burns dropped into a chair with a sigh of relief. Already, at a rough estimate, he'd done an eight-hour day. 'Well,' he said, 'what tidings do you bring from York, Sergeant?'

'I think we can forget that mileage problem, sir.'

'I'm glad to hear it . . . What's the explanation?'

'Just a bit of carelessness on the part of a garage hand, I'd say.' Ryder reported on his morning's visit to Fleetway Cars.

'Can I see the service book?' Burns asked.

Ryder passed it to him. Burns studied it for a moment. Then he said: 'This suggestion of yours that the figure should have been 36,301—that's just a guess, of course?'

'Yes—but it's quite a possible misreading. And the lower figure fits in with the mileage we know about.'

'You've worked it out, have you?'

'Yes, sir.' Ryder referred to his jottings. 'If we start with an actual mileage at the time of service of 36,301, and add twelve miles for the journey from the garage to the hotel, and ninety-five miles for the journey from the hotel to Lowark—which is what it is, give or take a mile or two—we get an expected mileage of 36,408. In fact, the mileage at Lowark was 36,459—fifty-one miles more. Which could easily be accounted for by the trip Quarry took round the moors on Saturday afternoon—plus, maybe, a slightly longer route to Lowark than the one I measured . . . It seems the obvious answer.'

'I suppose so,' Burns said, slowly. 'I certainly can't think of any other. All the same, I wish people wouldn't make these mistakes—the case is quite difficult enough as it is . . . Have you had the autopsy report yet?'

'Not the written report, sir, but I had a word with Carson when I got back. I can give you the main points, if you'd like.'

'Yes—go ahead.'

Ryder produced some notes. 'Well, Quarry was a fine physical specimen, very healthy, exceptionally powerful. The cause of death was asphyxia. There were indications of severe pressure on the windpipe, caused by some flattish object, possibly a shoe or a knee, after unconsciousness had resulted from a succession of blows on the head by a blunt, soft instrument.'

'A soft instrument?'

'Like a sandbag, Carson said.'

'Ah! So he was knocked out, and then his windpipe was deliberately trodden on or knelt on until he was dead?'

'That seems to be about it, sir.'

'H'm. Pretty brutal . . . Any other injuries?'

'A few bruises on the shoulders—perhaps caused by some of the blows missing their target. Bruising on the left knee—possibly the result of falling. Bruising on the right hand—possibly sustained when warding off blows.'

'Any bruises on the arm that was under the boot lid?'

'None at all, sir.'

Burns nodded. 'As we expected . . . What about time of death?'

'Between two and three o'clock yesterday morning. For once, Carson is definite—and it fits with the clock.'

'Well, it's nice to have one solid fact to go on . . . Did Carson find any physical traces of the assailant?'

'Nothing so far. No skin under the dead man's nails, or anything like that. No blood. I've sent Quarry's clothes to the lab. for checking.'

'Good . . . That's all, is it?'

'The post-mortem stains indicate that the body was put into the boot very soon after death, and not subsequently moved. That's the lot.'

'Well, it's quite a good report,' Burns said. 'More helpful than we usually get from Carson. Now—what did you find in the car?'

'I've got everything next door, sir. Perhaps you'd like to come in and take a look.'

Burns followed the sergeant into an adjoining office. There, on a long table, Ryder had set out all the contents of the Rover, duly identified and labelled.

'These things were in the glove compartment,' the sergeant said, pointing. 'These were on the back seat. These were on the floor or under the seats. They've all been checked for fingerprints, and photographed.'

Burns inspected the collection. It was a curious little assortment. In addition to the pennies, the pebble and the lump of putty that Ryder had already mentioned, there was a packet of sticking plaster, a bottle of Disprin, a tin of sweets, a small solid-rubber ball, an empty cigarette packet, a Biro pen, a pocket comb, a bottle-opener, a corkscrew, a man's folded white handkerchief with an R in the corner, and a variety of books, maps and guides.

'Any prints on the putty?' Burns asked.

'Yes, sir—a man's. Unidentified. One of the demonstrator's, I suppose.'

'And on the pebble?'

'Also a man's. Two clear prints. No one we know.'

Burns pointed to the ball. 'And that . . . Any tooth marks on it?'

'Tooth marks? No, sir—why?'

'I wondered if Quarry had a dog—not that I saw any signs of one at his house . . . Or is it another missile?'

'It could be,' Ryder said. 'But I'd guess it was a kid's ball.'

'Quarry didn't have any children—as far as we know.'

'No, but he probably knew some. Most people do. Kids from next door, perhaps.'

'Are there any prints on it?'

'Yes—a man's second and third fingers, right hand. Quite clear. Not Quarry's. Unidentified.'

Burns grunted. 'Where did you find it?'

Ryder looked at the label. 'On the floor, sir—under the front passenger-seat.'

'M'm . . . Well, it still strikes me as an odd thing for a man like Quarry to have in his car.'

Ryder said, 'I reckon most cars have some odd things in them, sir. My wife once found a baby's knitted bonnet in ours. Quite embarrassing, it was—I could never explain it.'

Burns smiled. 'Very wise of you, Sergeant . . . Right—we'd better have all this junk stored for the time being . . . Has Constable Williams reported on those hikers yet?'

'Not yet, sir—he's having a bit of trouble, I gather. The old boy—Watson—wasn't at home when he called. He's still chasing him up.'

'I see.' Burns led the way back to the main office. 'Well, that seems to take care of your end of things. Now I'd better bring you up to date about the Driscolls and Sullivan . . .'

Chapter Eight

An hour had passed. An hour during which Burns had done most of the talking and telling.

Now he was cleaning his pipe. It was one that Alice had given him for his last birthday, because there'd been a big cancer scare on at the time and this particular pipe was supposed to be hygienic and safe. It had a bowl that unscrewed, an aluminium barrel that detached, and a mouthpiece with an ingenious system of ducts. To smoke it, a countdown of space proportions was required. Like the routine of shaving and bathing, the process involved mechanical actions that aided clarity of thought. And, with all available information exchanged between the policemen, the time seemed to have arrived for thought that led to conclusions. Notably, on how the dead man had come to be at Lowark.

'Let's start with Quarry at the Moor View Hotel on Saturday night,' Burns said, unscrewing the bowl. 'It would appear from the evidence, wouldn't it, that when he went to bed just before eleven o'clock he had every intention of staying there?'

'Without a doubt, sir.'

'So that leaves us with a choice. Either something suddenly occurred to him while he was lying there—something he'd overlooked, some recollection—which made him change his mind. Or else he was removed, forcibly or persuasively, by someone else.'

'That's right,' Ryder said. 'And it's hard to see why he should have changed his mind. As far as we know, he'd had a restful weekend at the hotel, with nothing to worry him or upset him. He hadn't been disturbed by any phone calls or messages or visitors. He'd seemed relaxed and cheerful all the time. He'd just enjoyed a nightcap and he'd settled down with a book. It doesn't sound to me the sort of situation where you'd get a sudden change of mind. There'd have had to be something to trigger it off—and there wasn't anything. I'd go along with Driscoll on this.'

'You mean you think he was abducted?'

'I do, sir. If a man's in bed and quietly reading just before 11 p.m., and by 2.30 a.m. he's been murdered and his body's later found ninety-five miles away, in my book that adds up to a kidnapping.'

Burns nodded. 'Everything points that way, certainly . . . All right, let's consider how it might have happened, step by step. Get your imagination to work, Sergeant. I need something to chew on.'

'Okay,' Ryder said. He gazed at the ceiling for a moment, evidently found inspiration there, and said with vigour, 'Well, there's this villain who's decided to get rid of Quarry. He has his own car, and he follows Quarry from Lowark to the hotel. When he gets there, he finds out how long Quarry plans to stay, and in which room.'

'How?'

'Maybe he overhears the conversation between Quarry and Lady What's-her-name. Quarry probably doesn't know him by sight, so he can hang about for a while without arousing any suspicion. Waiting to order tea or something. Or else he just watches Quarry's movements and sees which room he goes to. No problem there, I'd say.'

'All right . . . Go on.'

'After that he does a bit of a recce around the place, checking up on the annexe and the path under the windows and maybe the car-park arrangements. Then he clears off, and puts up in some different pub—a pub in York, say, where he'll pass unobserved—till Saturday.'

'Why does he wait till Saturday? What's wrong with Friday?'

'His plans aren't complete, sir.' Ryder sounded very positive. 'For one thing, he's got to find a suitable place to leave his own car while he disposes of Quarry. He needs daylight for that. And since he knows that Quarry is going to stay for two nights, he's in no hurry.'

'Sounds reasonable,' Burns said, peering through the stem of his pipe as though it were a gun barrel. 'So he hangs about until Saturday evening, perfecting his plans. Then what?'

'He parks his car in the quiet spot he's chosen, within walking distance of the hotel. At eleven o'clock, or soon after, when all the guests have turned in, he sneaks up the drive and round the back of the annexe. He creeps up to Quarry's window. It's open, and the curtains are blowing, and he can see in. He sticks a gun through the gap and tells Quarry to keep his mouth shut and do as he's told or else.'

'What if the window *hadn't* been open?'

'It's a warm night, and there's no other ventilation, so it has to be.'

'I see . . .'

'He makes Quarry get up and dress. He switches off the lights, so they won't attract attention. He forces Quarry to climb out of the window, with the gun in his back—safer than leaving by the corridor, and almost as easy—and he marches him to the Rover.'

'So far, so good,' Burns agreed. 'And then . . .?'

'Then he tells Quarry to get in behind the wheel and drive to Lowark. The Rover leaves noiselessly because the drive and the lane both slope downhill—the car just trickles away in neutral. The villain sits in the back with the gun, to guard against any funny business. They reach the track just before 2.30. As the car stops, the villain assaults Quarry, knocks him unconscious after a heck of a struggle, and finishes the job outside the car by stamping on his throat. Then he loads the body into the boot, and scarpers.'

'I see you're postulating a big, strong man.'

'Sure.'

'Why doesn't he shoot Quarry with his gun?'

'Too noisy, sir. Or maybe he thinks the gun might be traced to him.'

'H'm . . . Well, your reconstruction's okay up to a point—but there are a few weaknesses. For instance, if Quarry had driven the car, his prints would have been all over the wheel. And they weren't—the wheel was smudged, except for the two prints at the top. That suggests to me that whoever drove the car was wearing gloves. The murderer, in fact. And he certainly wouldn't have driven it with Quarry conscious beside him . . . How do we get out of that?'

Ryder frowned. 'Yes, that is a snag . . . It looks as though we might have to bring in an accomplice.'

'I'd prefer to keep it to one villain at the moment, if we can.'

'Then I guess we backtrack, sir. What happened was that when the villain got Quarry to the Rover, he bumped him off right there on the spot. And then drove the body to Lowark.'

'After they'd struggled and wrecked the car in the drive.'

'That's right. You told me it was parked a long way from the hotel—so it's quite likely no one would have heard anything.'

'This must have happened at half-past two—because that's when Quarry died.'

'Yes, sir. Revised timetable—the villain showed up at the hotel later than we reckoned.'

'In which case he'd probably have found Quarry asleep.'

'Probably. That would have made things easier for him. He climbed in and woke Quarry with the gun.'

'Where was the murder weapon at this time? The sandbag, or whatever it was.'

'The villain had brought it up from his car and dumped it by the Rover. All ready for picking up and bashing Quarry with as he turned and started to get in.'

'M'm . . . What happened about the murderer's *own* car?'

'Well, for all we know,' Ryder said, 'it could still be up near the hotel. Or he could have gone back in his own time and collected it. Yesterday, or to-day. It'd have been a bit of a cross-country journey for him, but no real problem. If he'd had an accomplice, of course, the second man could have driven the car back.'

Burns nodded. 'But, theoretically, one man could have done the whole job on his own.'

'I should think so, sir. If he was tough enough and determined enough. What's your view?'

'I think you've shown it would have been possible . . . Of course, there are several things the theory leaves unexplained.'

'Such as what, sir?'

'Such as the fact that the Rover was turned round on the track. I could understand it if Quarry had driven the car there himself as a free man—to meet someone, say. He might well have reversed it when he got there—he'd have had to do it at some time, to leave. But if he, or his body, was taken there by a murderer who meant to dump the car anyway, what would have been the sense in turning it round?'

'I can't answer that one,' Ryder said.

'Well, it's a small point, I suppose—but it does bother me a little. It seems such an extraordinary thing to have done . . . Anyhow, leaving that for the moment, we appear to agree that a kidnapping and murder by a single armed man is at least a feasible explanation of what happened. So now we come to the next question—the motive of this hypothetical man.'

'I'd have thought that was pretty obvious, sir.'

'You mean it was someone from the factory?'

'That's what it looks like.'

'That's what a lot of things point to, I know. The hatred. The threats. The chance of ending the strike by getting rid of Quarry. The brutal nature of the murder. The writing of "Bastard" on the car . . . But isn't it a bit *too* obvious?'

'How do you mean, sir?'

'Wouldn't the factory situation have been rather a gift for anyone with a different sort of motive?'

'Ah—I see . . .'

'I've been giving quite a bit of thought to this, Sergeant—and frankly I'm not impressed by this factory motive idea. Let me give you a few reasons. First, if the murder arose out of the row at the factory, why did the murderer bring Quarry *back* to Lowark—and so draw attention to the factory aspect? Wouldn't he have been more likely to dump the body as far away from Lowark as possible? Somewhere up in Yorkshire, for instance?'

'It's a point,' Ryder agreed.

'I think it's a big point. It suggests to me that the murderer was someone who knew about the row at the factory—but wasn't himself a worker there. Someone who was taking advantage of the trouble to set up a phoney motive. Using Lowark as a blind to confuse the investigation.'

Ryder gave a thoughtful nod.

'And writing "Bastard" would fit in with that very well,' Burns went on. 'Much better than it fits with a factory motive, in my view. After all, if you've just battered your boss to death there can't be a lot of extra satisfaction to be got from scrawling rude words about him. You've already expressed your opinion quite forcibly.'

Ryder grinned. 'True.'

'And that's not all . . . It seems pretty clear that our murderer wore gloves during the whole time he was operating. There were no prints where he wrote "Bastard", no prints on the steering wheel—and my guess is there'll be no prints in the room. That suggests to me that he was someone who thought he might be checked on—someone who had a very special reason to be careful. And—apart perhaps from Sullivan—I wouldn't have thought that that would have applied to any of the factory workers. With thirty thousand fingerprints between them, they'd have felt pretty secure in any case.'

'Yes . . .'

'But the main reason why I'm doubtful about this factory motive,' Burns said, 'is something quite different . . . Quarry could have been killed locally by a factory worker at any time without too much trouble. He didn't have a police guard—and he was often in the area, driving around in an easily recognizable car. He could have been waylaid anywhere, and bumped off. He didn't have to be followed all the way to Yorkshire and kidnapped. Followed, mind you, to what would have been an unknown destination, which might not even have been a hotel, which could have been some place entirely unsuitable for a kidnapping. The murderer certainly couldn't have known, if he was just a casual, spur-of-the-moment pursuer from the factory, that Quarry would settle down in an almost empty ground-floor annexe in a remote spot, so giving him the perfect opportunity. It was a chance in a thousand . . . *I* don't think it makes sense.'

'What are you suggesting, then, sir?'

'I'm suggesting that if Quarry *was* followed, it could hardly have been casual—that it was more likely done by someone who was already keeping an eye on him, someone who'd worked out a murder plan and was patiently waiting for the right opportunity to carry it out . . . Alternatively, the murderer could have been someone who didn't need to do any following, because he *knew* where Quarry was staying last weekend. In either case, I'd expect the motive to have been a personal and private one.'

'Well, that's certainly a change of angle,' Ryder said. 'I wonder how many people did know where Quarry was staying.' He paused. 'Are you thinking about Driscoll, by any chance?'

'I'm prepared to give him a passing glance, Sergeant. What do *you* think about him?'

'I suppose a case could be made against him, sir. Quite a strong one, as a matter of fact. He was in a good position to see the value of the factory motive as a blind. He was recommending that motive to you when he saw you. He knew all about Quarry's movements. He knew the number of his room, and that it was in the annexe—and he might well have been familiar with the hotel. We know he owns a gun, which a kidnapper would have needed. And we know he was supposed to have been alone at his cottage on Saturday night—so he'd have had the opportunity.'

'All quite true,' Burns said, 'and very well put . . . But he hadn't any motive himself—as far as we know. He showed no signs of having recently been in a fight. He actually volunteered the information that he knew Quarry's room number and had called there—otherwise it's quite likely no one would have known. Rather a foolish thing to do, if he'd kidnapped and murdered Quarry during the night . . . And if Driscoll had taken Quarry to Lowark in the Rover, how would he have got back to Yorkshire in time for breakfast, without a car?'

Ryder considered, then nodded ruefully. 'So much for an impressive case! It seems to me, sir, we're just floundering at the moment.'

'I'm afraid we are,' Burns said. 'About the only thing we know for certain is that Quarry had an enemy, who bumped him off at 2.30 on Sunday morning. We don't know where it happened and we don't know the circumstances. We've no idea of the motive—it could have been anything. Money, a grudge, a woman, frustrated ambition, revenge—the field's wide open . . . What I'm sure about is that we should stop concentrating on the factory aspect, and extend our inquiries. I think we should go in search of muddy waters, and scoop around a bit, and see if anything comes up in the net.'

'All right, sir. Where do we start?'

'London,' Burns said. 'The head office of the company. Correspondence files. Quarry's colleagues. His will. His personal life. All that sort of thing . . . We'll drive up first thing in the morning, Sergeant, and get to work.'

PART TWO

Chapter One

The late Robert Quarry's personal assistant ushered Ryder into a rather magnificent panelled room and indicated a solid, leather-upholstered chair behind a massive mahogany desk. 'You should be comfortable here, Sergeant,' she said. 'It's Mr Quarry's old room. The files are over there when you're ready to look at them.' She indicated a row of steel cabinets and stood waiting, very composed and reserved, for any instructions. She was an eye-catching girl in her mid-twenties, dark, slim and svelte, but with an air of cool efficiency. Her name was Heather Johns.

Ryder glanced around, grinned, and said, 'Well, it's a bit rough but I guess I'll get by!' There hadn't been much opportunity for light-hearted badinage in this case so far—and now he saw there wasn't going to be much in the future. Miss Johns didn't even smile. There was a dazzling sparkle from a diamond on her engagement finger, but no responsive gleam in her eye. Perhaps, Ryder thought, she was still sad about her late boss . . .

The two policemen had driven up early that morning in separate cars, so that they could pursue their inquiries independently. The company secretary at Crowthers had been advised by telephone of the facilities that would be needed, and a note had been circulated to all departments saying that the police were to be given maximum assistance. Burns had worked out a division of labour for the first day or so. Ryder was to concentrate on the office staff, with a free hand to follow up anything that looked interesting. The superintendent was to see Quarry's solicitor, and then go on to Harpenden to try and get more background information from

Alma. The two of them would meet at their hotel each evening and pool their discoveries, if any.

Ryder said, 'Have a seat, Miss Johns. I'd like to talk to you.'

Miss Johns hesitated. 'I'm rather busy, you know . . .'

'We're *all* busy,' Ryder said. 'I'll only keep you a few minutes.'

The girl drew up a chair.

'How long have you been Mr Quarry's personal assistant?' In Ryder's own ears the question sounded a little abrupt—but though he'd sought to model himself on Burns, he hadn't yet achieved the superintendent's tactful felicity of phrase.

'About three years,' Miss Johns said.

'You knew him for quite a while before he was married, then?'

'Yes.'

'Where did he live at that time?'

'He had a flat in St John's Wood.'

'And a housekeeper?'

'No, it was a service flat. Someone went in each day and cleaned. And there was a restaurant downstairs.'

'I see. I'm only asking because I'm interested in his way of life at that time. How he occupied himself, what people he knew, and so on. Outside his work, I mean. It's not just idle curiosity. I need to build up a picture, and I'd be glad if you could help me.' (Yes—that was more like Burns!)

Miss Johns thawed a little. 'Well, he was so engrossed in the company's affairs, he didn't really have time for much else. He sometimes dined at his club, the Travellers, and met people there. And of course he entertained his friends occasionally.'

'Girl-friends?'

Miss Johns froze again. 'I wouldn't know about that. His private life was his own business.'

'Let's stick to his men friends, then. Who were his buddies?'

'He hadn't any "buddies",' Miss Johns said. 'He was a rather aloof man . . . I suppose his closest friend was Mr Driscoll—they'd known each other from early days. Otherwise he just had acquaintances—the people he sometimes played golf with, and so on. Of course, he used to visit his father fairly often—they liked to play chess at the weekends. They were both very keen players.'

'I hadn't heard about his father,' Ryder said.

'He had a house in Highgate. He was a widower—a housekeeper looked after him. He was very old—nearly eighty. And he had a slight stroke just before Mr Quarry married, which put an end to the chess games. But Mr Quarry continued to visit him, with his wife, until he died a few months ago.'

Ryder nodded. 'Are there any other relatives around?'

'There's a married niece, I believe.'

'Ah! Has she any children?'

'I don't know. Mr Quarry never talked about her. I don't think he had much to do with her.'

'I see. Well, from what you tell me, Mr Quarry led a fairly normal and uneventful existence before his marriage. Do you know of anything in his private life at that time that might have accounted for someone wanting to murder him?'

'Certainly not,' said Miss Johns.

'Right. Now let's move on to last weekend. What did he tell you about his plans? Anything?'

'He told me he was going to see Mr Driscoll about the strike—and that they were going shooting together. And he said he hoped to have a night or two in some quiet hotel.'

'But he didn't know where?'

'Not before he left. But he rang me on Friday and told me where he'd booked in.'

'Oh, he did?'

'Yes, of course. With all the trouble over the strike, he couldn't just disappear for a weekend without letting anyone know where he was. He might have been needed urgently.'

'What time did he ring you?'

'It must have been just before half-past five.'

'Did he say where he was ringing from?'

'Yes, from York.'

'What were you supposed to do with the information? Anything?'

'He asked me to let the vice-chairman know where he could be found. That's all.'

'Which you did?'

'Yes—I typed a memo and put it on his desk.'

'Did you keep a copy?'

'Yes. I keep copies of everything.'

'What did you do with your copy?'

'I put it in a file.'

'What did you do with the file?'

'I left it on my table. There was nothing important in it.'

'And then, I suppose, you went home?'

'Yes.'

Ryder nodded. 'Well, thank you, Miss Johns. I think that's all for now.'

Rather thoughtfully, he watched her leave. He was wondering just how personal her relationship had been with Quarry in the pre-Alma years; why she'd seemed so reluctant to talk about him; whether her engagement had preceded or followed the marriage . . . In fact, whether he ought to have probed a bit more, or whether that would have been an unwarranted intrusion considering that she certainly wasn't under suspicion of anything . . .

He was also thinking that with those two memos lying around in the office on Friday evening, anyone who'd happened to be working late could have learned where Quarry was spending the weekend . . .

Chapter Two

Burns sato, 'How much was he worth, Mr Landon?' He was sitting back comfortably in an old-fashioned chair in the somewhat dingy office of Landon, Holmes & Co., in Essex Street—the firm Miss Johns had named to him as Quarry's solicitors.

Landon, a Pickwickian figure nearing retiring age, said, 'At a rough guess, Superintendent, I'd say upwards of £450,000—before death duties.'

'As much as that?' Burns had expected something large, but nothing on that scale.

'Something of that order . . . Of course, in these inflationary days it sounds more than it is. A pleasant freehold house with an acre or two can easily be worth fifty thousand . . . Still, I agree it's a tidy sum.'

'And I assume Mr Quarry willed the bulk of it to his wife?'

'On the contrary,' Landon said, with a rather impish gleam, 'he died intestate.'

Burns stared at him in amazement. 'How on earth did that happen?'

'It's quite a complex story.'

'I'd very much like to hear it.'

'Well—until a few years ago Mr Quarry hadn't bothered to make a will at all. For one thing, he was in robust health and he thought he'd live for ever. For another, he had no dependants—and no charitable causes near his heart. His old father was well-to-do, and almost certain to pre-decease him. His brother, who lived in Canada, had been drowned in a boating accident. Quarry's only other blood relative was a married niece, a Mrs Angela Bellamy, née Angela

Quarry, whom he'd seen almost nothing of. So he said he'd wait for a while . . . Well, I managed to talk him out of that attitude. I pointed out, as any solicitor would, that if he didn't make a will, and anything happened to him, he might well be handing over a lot of money quite unnecessarily to a grasping Exchequer—which didn't appeal to him much. So finally, with a few suggestions from me, he did make a will. He left some fairly substantial sums to various institutions—to a hospital that had treated him after he was wounded in 1945, to his old school, and to his club—and the residue to his niece, Mrs Bellamy.'

Burns nodded. 'Most interesting. Please go on.'

'Well, that was all very well until he got married. Then, of course, he was anxious to change his will. He'd acquired a dependant—a young wife—and he expected children. So when he got back from his honeymoon at the beginning of this year he came straight along to me with Mrs Quarry—an exquisite lady, I may say— and asked me to draw up a new will. He cut out all the charitable bequests, which had never very much appealed to him; he left a generous £20,000 to the niece he hardly knew; and of course the very large residue went to his wife. He returned a few days later to sign the will, and he left it in my keeping.'

'That all seems very normal,' Burns said. 'So what happened?'

'Well, a couple of months or so ago he rang me up and asked me to post the will to him—which I did. A week later he rang me again and said he'd destroyed the will and wanted to make another one. Naturally I asked him why—I'd known him, you must remember, for many years—and he said he'd changed his mind about leaving anything to his niece. Apparently—though he hadn't realized it—she was a politically-minded young woman and very left-wing—in fact, quite extreme. She'd married an American student who was mixed up with Black Panthers, and they'd both been arrested during some demonstration while they were on a visit to the United States, and fined. Quarry had read about it in a newspaper, and had taken a very poor view indeed—he, of course, was on the Right in politics—and he didn't see why he should subsidize revolution. So he wanted to cut the girl out of his will.'

'That makes sense,' Burns said. 'And then . . .?'

Landon threw out his hands expressively. 'Then he was murdered.'

'Before he got around to making the change.'

'Exactly. And as he'd been unwise enough to destroy his old will, he died intestate.'

'That's quite a remarkable story,' Burns said.

'It is, isn't it? The irony is, of course, that what will happen now is the very opposite of what Quarry wanted. Under the law of intestacy, his niece will get a very substantial slice of the estate.'

'So, in simple terms, Mrs Bellamy benefited financially by Quarry's death, and Mrs Quarry suffered.'

'That's exactly the position.'

'M'm . . .' Burns pondered. 'Do you happen to know where the Bellamys are living?'

'I think the last address I had for them was in Wembley.' Landon went to a cabinet, and picked out a card. 'Yes, here we are—6 Clover Court, Wembley.'

'Thank you,' Burns said. 'And I'm much obliged to you for your help.'

He left rather thoughtfully. His inquiries had undoubtedly produced a possible personal motive for murder—but only if Angela Bellamy and her husband had known about the various moves in the will affair. Which seemed, on the whole, highly improbable . . .

Still, it might be as well to look into their activities.

Chapter Three

Sergeant Ryder was sitting in a small anteroom at Crowthers occupied by Miss Frey, the vice-chairman's secretary. Burns' parting word of advice to him had been 'Don't hesitate to go to the top—it's always a good place to start.' Which was why Ryder was now waiting for the vice-chairman, a man named Alexander Baird, to return from a board meeting upstairs. The time was around noon.

He didn't have to wait long. The vice-chairman came in at a quarter past twelve, looking rather pleased with himself. He was a heavily-built man in his middle forties, dark-suited and wearing an Old Harrovian tie. He had a broad, fleshy face under a widow's peak of thinning dark hair, and looked as though he took more calories than exercise. But his air of physical indolence was more than offset by a shrewdly alert expression. Behind the thick-rimmed glasses he wore, there was the glint of a very sharp intelligence.

'I won't keep you a moment,' he said to Ryder, and beckoned his secretary to follow him into his office. When she emerged a minute or two later, she also looked extremely pleased. 'Mr Baird will see you now,' she said—and added, in a confidential whisper, 'He's just been made chairman of the company.'

'Is that so!' Ryder grinned. 'Then I'll go in on tiptoe!' He went in, and took the chair Baird indicated. The new head of the firm gave him a keen glance—focusing, it seemed, on the young sergeant's trendy dress and modish sideburns.

'Well,' Baird said, 'I'm at your disposal. What is it you want to ask me?'

Ryder explained the position. 'We're interested, sir, in anyone—anyone at all—who might appear to have had a motive for killing Robert Quarry . . . Excluding, that is, the factory workers at Lowark.'

'Why exclude them?'

'A policy decision,' Ryder said. 'It's a little complex . . .'

'I'm accustomed to complexities, Sergeant.'

'I'm sure, sir—but for the moment I'd prefer not to go into that. I'm concerned just now with personal situations—particularly in this office. Do you happen to know if Mr Quarry was involved in any personal quarrels here—any serious personal disputes? Was there anyone, would you say, with a special grudge against him?'

'In a big office,' Baird said, 'there are always grudges—but they don't as a rule lead to murder . . .' He frowned. 'As it happens, Mr Quarry *was* involved in a bit of unpleasantness a short time ago—but I'm quite sure it's irrelevant to his death.'

'May I have the details, sir?'

'Well, we had a man here named Walter Wharton—a man of about thirty-five, I suppose. He'd been with us as a clerk for ten years. He was a strange character—efficient enough in his work, but with a chip on his shoulder as big as a tree . . . About three weeks ago, someone sent the chairman an article clipped from a leftwing review. It was on the subject of the Lowark strike. It was very hostile to the management, and to Mr Quarry personally—and it also showed knowledge of confidential company matters. It was signed with a pen name, but internal evidence suggested that it might have been written by Wharton. Quarry tackled him, and he admitted it. He was sacked on the spot for disloyalty, without references.'

'By Quarry?'

'Yes, by Mr Quarry personally. The Board subsequently approved, of course—it was a bad case. Not that they had much choice, to be honest,'

'How was that, sir?'

'Well, Mr Quarry was a bit of a despot, you know—he liked to have his own way. If there'd been any serious opposition, he'd have been quite capable of resigning his chairmanship on the spot . . . He was a very dominating man, Robert Quarry.'

'It doesn't sound as though you wholly approved of him, sir.'

'I admired his drive arid ability, but I won't pretend he was an easy man to get on with . . . Anyhow, that's the position about Wharton—though as far as murder's concerned I wouldn't have thought he was worth a second glance.'

'I'll have to check, sir, all the same. It's sometimes surprising, the people who turn out to be capable of murder. Do you know his address?'

'I don't—but I'm sure Miss Johns will be able to give it to you.'

Ryder nodded. 'I'll ask her. Now, have there been any other incidents? Can you think of anyone else with a possible grudge?'

'No one in the office,' Baird said. 'But I seem to remember Quarry had some trouble a year or two back over a man he gave evidence against in court. Some motoring offence, I think. Again, you could probably get the details from Miss Johns. It's a long time ago, though—I wouldn't imagine that that has any relevance, either.'

'Well, thank you, sir—you've been quite a help.'

Baird glanced at his watch. 'Is that all, Sergeant?'

Ryder hesitated. There was a question he felt he ought to ask. It was a question, he was sure, that Burns would have asked. What was the phrase Burns had used—"frustrated ambition"? And, after all, he'd been given a free hand. He braced himself.

'There is just one thing, sir. I wonder if you'd mind telling me where you were last Saturday night?'

There was a little silence. Then Baird said, 'That's a rather odd question, isn't it, Sergeant?'

'Just routine, sir.'

'What do you mean—routine? I assume you're not going around asking everyone you meet where they were last Saturday night?'

'Not everyone, sir.'

'Then why me?'

Ryder almost wished he hadn't asked the question—but it was too late to withdraw now. He sought for a tactful way of explaining—and failed to find one. 'Robert Quarry,' he said, 'was killed on Saturday night, as you know. We're interested in the movements of anyone who might have had a motive for killing him. I understand you have now become chairman of the company in Quarry's place . . . As I say, it's a routine question.'

Baird's sharp eyes glinted behind their glasses. 'Don't you think you're rather exceeding your duty, Sergeant?'

'I don't, sir.'

'It doesn't strike you as an impudent question?'

'Not at all, sir.'

'H'm . . .' Baird flicked a switch at his side. 'Miss Frey—get me the Commissioner of Police on the line, will you?' He sat back, regarding Ryder with a sardonic smile.

Ryder stared down at the floor. Things didn't usually go as wrong as this. *Had* he exceeded his duty? He couldn't see why. A simple question, to an innocent man . . .

The phone rang. Baird lifted the receiver. 'Ah, Harold . . . Sorry to trouble you, but I've got a young detective-sergeant with me. Not one of your men—he's from the north. He's inquiring into the Quarry murder. He insists on knowing where I spent last Saturday evening. I thought it would be salutary if you had a word with him . . . Right . . .'

Baird passed the receiver to Ryder. 'Go ahead—talk to the commissioner.'

Ryder took the phone. 'Detective-Sergeant Ryder, sir—Nottinghamshire County Police'

A crisp voice said, 'This is Sir Harold Munro, Sergeant. Mr Baird dined with me last Saturday evening. He was with me until just before midnight. All right?'

'Thank you, sir.' Ryder put the phone back on its rest.

Baird got to his feet, smiling. 'Satisfied?'

Ryder was looking at the pad on Baird's desk. He had an urge to lean over, and follow the murderer's example, and scrawl 'Bastard' on it. Instead, he said, 'Perfectly satisfied, sir'—and left.

Chapter Four

After seeing the solicitor, Burns drove straight out to Wembley, which happened to be conveniently on his route to Harpenden. If Robert Quarry's niece wasn't at home, he'd have lost little time.

Clover Court turned out to be a small block of rather run-down flats backing on to a railway. On the door of number 6 there was a slip of pasteboard with 'Bellamy' typed on it. Some odd thumping noises were coming from inside the flat. Burns knocked, and waited. In a few moments a woman opened the door. She was tall, needle-thin and fiftyish. A head-scarf was tied round her hair and she was holding a duster.

'Good afternoon,' Burns said. 'Is Mrs Angela Bellamy at home?'

The woman scrutinized him. 'I'm afraid not. I'm her mother-in-law. Can I help you?' Her accent was American.

Burns introduced himself. 'I'm inquiring into the death of her uncle, Mr Robert Quarry,' he said.

'Oh, my, wasn't that just terrible? I read about it in the paper . . . Won't you step inside, Mr Burns?'

'Thank you.' Burns followed her into a small sitting-room—and the cause of the thumping noises became apparent. There were piles of books and various other chattels stacked on the floor and on the furniture, and two large crates were in process of being filled.

'I'm sorry about the mess,' Mrs Bellamy said. 'Here, let me clear a chair for you.'

Burns checked her. 'Please don't trouble.'

'What did you want to see Angela about, Mr Burns?'

'I'm trying to gather all the information I can about Mr Quarry,' he told her. 'I thought perhaps his niece might be a useful source.'

Mrs Bellamy shook her head. 'I doubt that Angela would have been much help—she hardly knew her uncle. Anyway, you've missed her. She and Henry—that's my son—they've just flown out to Ghana, West Africa.'

'Oh—really? When did they go?'

'Noon on Sunday. They plan to work out there for a couple of years.'

'I see. And they left you to clear up, eh?'

'That's right.'

'Do *you* live over here, Mrs Bellamy?'

'No, my home's in Connecticut. I flew in on Friday to lend a hand and see them off, that's all.'

Burns nodded. 'You must have had a pretty busy weekend.'

'We sure did. Mind you, getting out of a furnished apartment isn't like moving house—but there was packing to do, and friends dropping by, and a farewell party Saturday night. We didn't get to bed till three.'

'M'm . . . What are your son and daughter-in-law going to do in Ghana, Mrs Bellamy?'

'Well, Henry's going to study conditions out there—he's been given a research grant by the Cleaver Foundation. And Angela's going to work for the Community Service Council in Accra.'

'Community Service Council . . . Is that a political organization?'

'It is not, Mr Burns. It's a genuine charity—no politics at all, I'm thankful to say.'

'You speak with feeling.'

'I've good reason, Mr Burns. Those two young people got in trouble back home—mixing with lefties and going to demos and talking about overthrowing society. They had me real bothered for a while. But that's all over—I guess it was mostly high spirits. Right now they're all set to do a useful job where it's needed. I don't reckon there'll be any more talk of revolution.'

Probably not, Burns thought—in view of the fortune that would soon be coming to Angela! He took a tentative step towards the door. 'Well, I'll obviously have to look elsewhere for information about Mr Quarry. I hope I haven't disturbed you too much—and thank you for talking to me.'

'You're very welcome,' Mrs Bellamy said.

Burns walked briskly back to his car. If Angela Bellamy and her husband had been having a farewell celebration on Saturday night and were on a plane for Accra by noon on Sunday, it was clear they were out of the case. All the same, he'd check with the airline . . .

Chapter Five

Sergeant Ryder went off that afternoon to interview the dismissed clerk, Walter Wharton. The address in West Hampstead that he'd been given by Miss Johns turned out to be a bachelor bed-sitter in a decayed mansion block. Wharton was at home. He was a small, wiry man, with crew-cut grey hair like steel wool, and startlingly blue eyes. He looked older than his thirty-five years. He showed no sign of any physical injuries, and in build he certainly didn't conform to the popular idea of a brutal murderer. But then, as the sergeant well knew, some of the most notorious killers by violence had been small, frail men, making up in cunning what they lacked in strength. Where crime was concerned, it was never entirely safe to judge by appearances.

Wharton's manner, from the moment Ryder explained his business, was peculiarly unpleasant. 'I suppose,' he said, 'you're looking for a scapegoat.' He held his head a little on one side as he talked, as though he was slightly deaf. His voice was plaintive. 'I might have known someone would point the finger at me after what happened. But it just means they don't know what I'm really like. I'd never have had the brains.'

'Nobody's accusing you of anything,' Ryder said. 'All I'm doing is making a routine inquiry about someone known to have been on bad terms with Robert Quarry. Perhaps you'd care to give me your own version of the trouble you had with him.'

Wharton did so. His account of his misfortune was low-keyed and told in a half-humorous way—but punctuated by a succession of derogatory comments about Quarry, Crowthers and the Board. His attitude was a particularly disagreeable mixture of self-denigration, self-pity and deliberate provocation. He wasn't complaining about what had been done to him, he said—it was the sort of thing you had to expect from a man like Quarry. He wasn't surprised that his politics had been held against him—that was the way the system worked; it was what they called living in a free country. He didn't particularly mind being on the dole—he was alone in the world and his requirements were few. He only ate to keep alive . . .

Ryder heard him out—though the effort was a strain on his patience. 'Right,' he said, as the monologue finished, 'now let's get down to brass tacks. I suppose you got your confidential information from the files?'

'That's very intelligent of you, Sergeant . . . Since I happened to be the filing clerk!'

'Did you also happen to overhear any of Quarry's plans before you left Crowthers? Any suggestion that he might be taking a weekend away in the near future?'

'How could I do that? I was never around with him—I wasn't important enough. I was just a bit of furniture in that office. Everyone sat on me.' Wharton looked rather pleased with his joke.

'Have you seen anyone from the office since you left?'

'Is it likely? No one would bother with me now.'

'Have you or haven't you?'

'No, I haven't.'

'Do you own a car?'

'Well—I don't know whether *you'd* call it a car. It's about ten years old. That's the only sort of car people in my position can afford.'

'I hadn't noticed,' Ryder said drily. 'What make is it?'

'A Morris Minor.'

'What colour?'

'Grey.'

'Where were you on Saturday night?'

'Ah—I thought that would be the next thing . . . I was at a party committee meeting. At the branch chairman's flat.'

'What's his name and where does he live?'

'His name's Frank Johnson. He lives at 129a West End Lane.'

'What time did the meeting break up?'

'About one o'clock in the morning. It was one of those long meetings that didn't get anywhere—at least, I didn't think so. I'm stupid, I suppose.'

'All right, Mr Wharton,' Ryder said, his patience at an end. 'That's all for now.'

He drove away somewhat gloomily. None of the people in this case had much appeal for him. There was Quarry himself—obviously he'd been an awkward, difficult man. There was the supercilious new chairman, Baird, taking the mickey. There was Miss Johns—fetching to look at, but far from amiable. And now this creep Wharton ... Still, he reflected, if you deliberately set out to interview people with grudges you were hardly likely to find them full of the joys of spring ...

There was no one at home at the Johnsons' flat when he got there, and he had to wait nearly an hour before anyone arrived. Then Mrs Johnson showed up, a massive woman breathless with exertion and shopping. She seemed to resent the sergeant's questions—at 129a West End Lane, policemen were evidently unwelcome. Why, she asked, should he be concerning himself with a political meeting? They weren't against the law, were they? And why was he so interested in Mr Wharton? What was Wallie supposed to have done? But in the end she gave way and answered the questions. Yes, there *had* been a party meeting on Saturday night. Yes, it *had* gone on till just before one o'clock. Yes, Wallie Wharton *had* been there—right to the end.

'Who else attended the meeting?' Ryder asked.

The nattering started again. What business was it of the police? Anyone would think the flat had been full of anarchists. They'd only been *talking* ... But finally Ryder got a name—a Miss Freda Hilton, a schoolteacher, who lived two blocks along the Lane. He called on her and found her, to his relief, a lively, good-looking girl who gave no trouble. Yes, she said at once, she'd been at the meeting and Mr Wharton had been there. In fact, he'd walked her home when the meeting had broken up.

So that, for the moment, appeared to be that. Not even Burns, Ryder thought, could have checked a story more conscientiously.

Chapter Six

Burns had driven to Harpenden, having telephoned Alma Quarry from a call-box in Wembley and proposed a visit. The Quarry home—and its environs—seemed to the superintendent as good a place as any for his own check on possible private enemies.

He was admitted by someone he hadn't seen before—a middle-aged woman who in reply to his inquiry said she was Mrs Waters and that she was Mrs Quarry's 'daily'. The Aspinalls, he learned from her, had left The Hillocks on Monday morning. Mrs Quarry, having recovered from the first shock of the murder, had preferred to face her tragedy alone.

Alma came out into the hall to greet him. She was pale and heavy-eyed, as though from lack of sleep, but her composed manner showed that the process of adjustment had begun. Grief had lost a little of its edge.

Burns apologized for this second intrusion, though in fact Alma made it clear that she was glad to see him. It was as though, in her bereavement, she needed some father-figure to rely on. He made some conventional inquiries about the funeral arrangements which would follow the inquest—set down, as he knew, for the following day. This was the twilight period, between the dead past and the more hopeful future ... He learned that the Aspinalls had taken charge of everything, that a funeral notice would be inserted in *The Times*, that the cards were ready to be sent out, that Alma herself had no immediate problems to cope with—and he moved on to business.

'The position, Mrs Quarry, is this,' he said. 'We need more help in trying to trace the man who killed your husband. We've considered the possibility of a motive arising from the factory strike, but—for various reasons that I won't trouble you with now—we think that that may not be the answer. We're now thinking in terms of a more personal motive—of something arising from the private circumstances of your husband's life. And this is where I hope you may be able to help us. Is there anyone you can think of who might have had a grudge against Mr Quarry? Anyone who might conceivably have wished to get rid of him for purely private reasons?'

Alma sat frowning. 'No,' she said after a moment, 'no one at all. We'd only been married for ten months, as I expect you know—but certainly during that time I never heard about anyone who might have had a grudge.'

'You never heard of any quarrel? With a neighbour, perhaps—a business acquaintance . . .? Any small incident that might give us a lead?'

Alma shook her head. 'There was nothing that I know of,' she repeated. 'Apart from the strike, I don't think Robert was troubled by anything . . . The strike did worry him, very much. He was angry about it, he couldn't sleep, it was on his mind day and night . . . But I never heard of anything else that worried him.'

'Are you sure about that, Mrs Quarry? I expect he talked to you sometimes about his life before he met you? A very adventurous life, I understand, during the war—and a very active and vigorous one since. Did he never refer to any incident in his past which, as you look back now, might possibly have led to this tragedy?'

'No,' Alma said. 'He did talk about the war sometimes, of course. He told me stories about his commando raids—and about the landings in France on D-day. He told me about men he'd killed—and how it had happened. He told me all sorts of things—personal things—his feelings—the way people do. It was all rather remote to me, because I hadn't even been born then . . . There may have been something before I knew him—something he kept secret, and that led to his murder. But if there was, it didn't show, it didn't seem to worry him. It didn't prevent him from being completely happy . . . Perhaps there was something that he himself didn't remember—I don't know . . . I really can't help you, I'm afraid.'

'I see . . . Well, there it is—I thought at least I ought to ask you.'

'John Driscoll would be much more likely to know than I would,' Alma said. 'He and Robert were friends for such a long time—they knew each other intimately. Years before I ever met either of them. I should ask John, if I were you.'

'Very well, I'll do that—I'll have another talk with him,' Burns paused for a moment. Then he said, 'Tell me, Mrs Quarry, did your husband have a study in the house? A place where he sometimes worked?'

'Yes—of course. Every man has to have some place of his own, doesn't he?'

'That's what I thought. I wonder if I might take a look there. At any papers there may be—at any correspondence? We badly need a lead—and sometimes old records can provide one.'

'You can look at anything you wish, Superintendent. Robert's study is the second door on the left at the top of the stairs. You'll find the keys to the files in his desk drawer, I think.'

'Thank you,' Burns said.

He climbed to the landing and entered the study. It was a small, intimate room, with a desk, a leather chair, a portable typewriter, a telephone extension, and two filing cabinets. Burns tried the keys, and after a little experimenting he found the one that fitted the cabinets. He removed a tray, and sat down at the desk to go through the contents.

The papers, he found, were mostly of a domestic nature. Quarry had evidently preferred to handle his personal affairs without the intervention of a secretary. There were local bills and receipts, correspondence with a builder about the decoration of the house, correspondence about the possible construction of a swimming-pool in the grounds, correspondence with a firm of valuers about the insurance of a diamond brooch. There were also carbon copies of some business letters which Quarry appeared to have typed himself. One of them was addressed to a firm of stockbrokers in Cornhill—Keenan, Hall & Webb—and the tone of it at once caught Burns' attention. It was dated September 17th of the current year, and it read:

Dear Sirs,

I refer to the member of your firm, Mr Peter Saxon, who has been advising me about my investment portfolio.

I was far from impressed by Mr Saxon's review of the stock market situation when, at my request, he visited me at my home on August 7th. I am even less satisfied now, following the disastrous fall in Electronic Products, which he strongly recommended as a growth company. I am surprised that a firm of your standing should employ a man who would appear to be so lacking in the basic qualifications for the job. In view of what happened I am terminating my connection with your firm, and would be obliged if you would return to me any outstanding share certificates. I await your final account for settlement.

Yours faithfully,
Robert Quarry

Attached to the copy was the reply of the stock-broking firm. It read:

Dear Sir,

We note the contents of your letter of September 17th, and regret very much that our Mr Saxon has not given you satisfaction. We have always found Mr Saxon a most reliable and conscientious member of the firm, and we have the highest regard for his ability. You will appreciate that advice about the future movements of shares must always be subject to error, since none of us is clairvoyant. It would be possible for us to suggest a substitute for Mr Saxon in the handling of your affairs, but in view of the evident loss of confidence in our firm that your letter indicates we agree that it might be in the better interests of all concerned if the connection were ended. We therefore enclose the share certificates relating to recently-discussed changes in your portfolio, together with our terminal account.

Yours faithfully,
A. D. Richards

Burns looked at the letter heading. Richards was named as one of the partners. Saxon was not. Presumably he was a fairly junior member of the firm. The tone of the correspondence, Burns thought, was surprisingly sharp. Particularly the tone of Quarry's letter—it sounded positively vindictive. If that was his normal way of conducting business, it wasn't surprising that he'd made enemies . . .

Burns put the letters aside, and continued reading. But nothing else of particular note emerged, and eventually he went downstairs, taking the two letters with him. Alma was listening to a concert on the radio, but not with any deep concentration. She switched it off at Burns' approach, and he showed her the letters. 'Your husband seems to have been involved in a dispute with his stockbrokers,' he said. 'Do you know anything about it?'

Alma read through the correspondence, and shook her head. 'I'm afraid it means absolutely nothing to me,' she said. 'Robert never discussed his business affairs with me. He knew I wouldn't understand them.'

'But you probably remember this man Peter Saxon? It seems he came here once.'

'Saxon . . . Oh, yes, he called here one Saturday. Robert had made a special appointment with him.'

'What impression did you have of him, Mrs Quarry?'

'None, to speak of . . . He was a young man—quite good-looking—very polite. I only saw him for a moment or two, when I let him in . . . You're surely not thinking *he* might have borne a grudge?'

'I'm considering possibilities—nothing more.'

‘Well, you could always go and see him, I suppose.’

‘Yes,’ Burns said. ‘When I’ve cleared up Mr Quarry’s papers, I think I will.’

Chapter Seven

Having been provided by Miss Johns with some particulars of the man Robert Quarry had given evidence against, and by Scotland Yard with the essential details of the case, Sergeant Ryder made his last call that day on a certain George Adams—described in a charge-sheet some eighteen months earlier as a journalist, 31, of Glebe Street, Pimlico.

Adams had, in fact, been a highly-paid reporter on a Sunday newspaper. Driving along Pall Mall one evening after dark, he had knocked down and killed a man on a pedestrian crossing. His defence had been that the man had shown no sign of stepping off the pavement until avoiding action was impossible. There had been two chief prosecution witnesses. One, a woman, had given evidence that the dead man had already been well out on the crossing when he'd been hit. The other witness had been Robert Quarry, who had just come out of his club. Quarry had said that the dead man had been struck right in the middle of the crossing and that Adams had approached it at a speed of at least sixty miles an hour. His evidence, unshaken in cross-examination, had been accepted by the jury, and Adams had been sentenced to two years' imprisonment for manslaughter. He had been released just six weeks ago.

Ryder found him still living in Pimlico, though at a different address. He was a big man slimmed down by prison fare, to judge by the looseness of his clothes. He had a head of flaming red hair and a beard to match—and when he heard that Ryder was a policeman his temper flamed too. 'Good God,' he cried, 'am I always to be hounded?'

'No one's hounding you, sir,' Ryder said quietly. 'I'm merely seeking answers to a question or two.'

'What about?'

'The late Robert Quarry. You may have read that he was murdered?'

'Of course I did. Serve the bastard right! He added twenty miles an hour to the speed I was doing. He practically got me jailed single-handed. What am I supposed to do—go into mourning?'

'No, sir—and I'm not here to re-try the case. All I wish to know is where you were last Saturday.'

'Why?'

'It's a question I'm putting to everyone I can find who might have had a grudge against Quarry. Some people might think you had a considerable grudge.'

'Some people would be damned right! But if you imagine I had anything to do with his murder you're crazy.'

'It's a routine question, sir—nothing more. What were your movements on Saturday?'

'My movements?' Adams gave a loud guffaw. 'Oh, I like that. Sergeant, at three o'clock last Saturday I was getting *married*. My fiancée, bless her heart, was one of the few people who stood by me while I was in prison. We were married at Chelsea Register Office. Here, look for yourself.' He produced a certificate from a drawer and showed it to Ryder. 'Does that satisfy you?'

Ryder glanced at the certificate, which bore the appropriate date. 'Yes, I can't argue with that . . . No honeymoon, sir?'

'We couldn't afford a proper honeymoon. I haven't got a job yet—we can only just about pay the rent.'

'So where did you spend the night, sir?'

'On an island in the Blackwater river, in Essex. White-sea Island. An old friend lent us his bungalow there for the weekend.'

'What's the name of the friend?'

'Armitage. Harry Armitage.'

'You had the use of a boat, I take it?'

'No—just the bungalow.'

'Then how did you get out to the island?'

'There's a low-tide causeway. We drove across.'

'You have a car, have you?'

'*I* haven't. I had to sell mine, to pay for the trial costs. Anyway, I'm still disqualified from driving. But my wife has a car. In fact, I think she's just arrived in it.'

There was the sound of a key turning in the front door. In a moment a girl came in. She was tall, neatly dressed, and good-looking in a rather sharp-featured way. She was wearing a bright new wedding ring. 'Hello, darling,' she said—and glanced inquiringly at Ryder.

'A policeman, Jackie.'

'Oh? Why?'

'Some nonsense about that fellow Quarry. The sergeant's been asking me where I was on Saturday night. I told him we were on the island—but I'm not sure he believes me.'

The girl looked at Ryder in surprise. 'Of course we were. We went down there on Saturday afternoon and stayed till Monday. Anyone on the island will tell you.'

'I see,' Ryder said. 'Well—thank you. That's all.'

As he made his way back to his car, he considered the pros and cons. Adams had certainly had a monumental grudge—and men with long memories did sometimes take their revenge ... A dangerously reckless driver was often a dangerously reckless man ... Adams had shown no signs of injuries—but all that face fungus might have concealed bruises ... His wife had supported his story—but the evidence of a wife was scarcely better than no evidence at all ... They'd certainly been married on Saturday—but there were more things than one you could do on your wedding night ... Especially if there was a causeway to the mainland ...

In short, Ryder wasn't satisfied ...

Chapter Eight

The stockbroker, Peter Saxon, had left his office by the time the superintendent got back to town from Harpenden, but a late-working switchboard girl supplied his home telephone number after a little pressure and Burns was able to make an immediate appointment to see him at his Finchley flat.

The flat, on the top floor of a well-preserved Victorian house, was spacious and comfortable without being at all luxurious. Saxon received Burns amiably. He was thirtyish, tall, of slight-to-average build, and very much at ease. Burns gave him a quick once-over, but could see no sign of any physical injury.

'Well, Superintendent, what's brought you here?' Saxon asked, as soon as they were seated.

'I'm investigating the murder of Robert Quarry,' Burns said. 'I'm making a routine check on everyone known to have been on bad terms with him.'

Saxon grinned. 'That sounds like a life's work! How did you get on to me?'

'I came across a letter about Quarry's investment affairs when I was at his home to-day. It was addressed to your firm, and it mentioned you. I gather you had trouble with him after a visit to his house in August.'

'I wouldn't say *I* had trouble with him,' Saxon said. 'The firm certainly did. *I* was more surprised than anything. Quarry had never made any complaints about me before, and he hadn't shown any particular signs of dissatisfaction when we'd talked about his affairs that morning—so his letter was rather a bolt from the blue.'

'But you felt some resentment, no doubt?'

'Not enough to want to bump him off, Superintendent, if that's what's in your mind. I thought his criticism quite unfair, and I was naturally peeved. But that's all. Life's too short to worry about the occasional bad-tempered client.'

'It was certainly short for him,' Burns said.

'Yes, indeed, poor chap.'

'His complaint was very strongly worded . . . As a matter of interest, did it do you any harm with your firm?'

'A complaint never does one any *good*, does it?' Saxon said. 'I was given a bit of a grilling by the senior partner—but I wouldn't say I suffered.'

'How long had you known Mr Quarry?'

'About two years.'

'Had you visited his house before?'

'No.'

'Had you a social relationship with him?'

'No—only a business relationship.'

'Business lunches, perhaps?'

'Not even that, Superintendent.'

'Too bad,' Burns said. 'I'd always imagined these captains of industry driving their stockbrokers to luxury inns at weekends for a profitable huddle over good food and expensive wine.'

Saxon shook his head. 'Not Quarry, I'm afraid. He drove me almost nuts—that's all the driving he ever did for me.'

'Where did you normally meet?'

'In his office. He expected everyone to dance attendance on him. I was one of the dancers.'

'How often did you meet?'

'Oh—perhaps once every three or four months, over a couple of years. We talked on the phone now and again, of course.'

'But after the row, I assume you didn't see him again.'

'You assume correctly, Superintendent.'

'M'm . . . Have you a car, Mr Saxon?'

'Yes—I've a Ford Escort.'

'Would you care to tell me what you were doing last Saturday night? Just for the record.'

'Saturday? Let me think ... Oh, yes, I took a girlfriend to the theatre. Let's Go Loving, at the Lyric. Not bad at all.'

'And afterwards?'

'I drove her home to Kensington and had a drink at her place.'

'How long did you stay?'

Saxon smiled wryly. 'Not as long as I'd have liked. She had a headache . . . I suppose until about eleven—eleven-fifteen. Something like that.'

'Then what?'

'Then I came back to Finchley and went to the Queen's—that's an after-theatre restaurant.'

'What time did you leave there?'

'Oh—some time after one.'

Burns nodded. 'Might I know the name and address of the young lady you took to the theatre?'

'I say, you *are* thorough. I really don't rate this attention, I assure you.'

'Probably not, Mr Saxon—but we have to go through the motions, you know.'

'I suppose you do ... Well, I don't imagine she'll mind. It's Miss Cynthia Hollis—Flat 6, Heritage Mansions, SW7. Her phone number's 937 00624. Perhaps you'd like to give her a ring now?'

'Thank you—I'd prefer to see her.' Burns picked up his bowler.

'She's a charming girl,' Saxon said. 'You'll like her.' He accompanied Burns to the door. 'Good luck with the leg work, Superintendent.'

Cynthia Hollis was a slim, attractive blonde in her early twenties, with a rather debby voice. Burns took to her at once.

'This is a purely routine check,' he told her, 'and there's absolutely nothing to worry about ... I understand that a Mr Peter Saxon was with you last Saturday evening.'

'Yes, he was,' Cynthia Hollis said. 'We went to the theatre.'

'Thank you, Miss Hollis. That's all I wanted to know.'

The Queen's Restaurant proved to be a very superior

establishment. Its menu offered exotic and expensive dishes at correspondingly high prices. Its bar was pleasant, its décor tasteful, its atmosphere serene. A discreet notice announced that it served after-theatre meals until 2 a.m., and advised reservations.

Burns sought out the owner, introduced himself, and went through his usual spiel. 'A simple routine inquiry, sir, no more . . . Do you happen to know a Mr Peter Saxon?'

The owner smiled. 'But, of course, Superintendent. Mr Saxon often comes here. He's a valued customer.'

'Can you tell me when he was here last?'

'Oh, quite recently . . . Let me see—yes, last Saturday evening.'

'What time did he arrive—roughly?'

'I should think about half-past eleven.'

'I see. And can you remember what time he left?'

'Ah . . .' The owner beckoned a waiter. 'What time did Mr Saxon leave on Saturday, Alex?'

'I believe, a little earlier than usual,' the waiter said, after a moments thought. 'I would say, just before half-past one.'

Burns nodded to them both. 'Well—thank you very much.'

'Mr Saxon is not any trouble, I hope,' the owner said, as Burns prepared to leave.

'None whatever,' Burns assured him—thinking to himself, 'I almost wish he was!'

Chapter Nine

When the two policemen met that evening and exchanged reports on their activities, Burns agreed that the only way of checking up conclusively on George Adams' story would be to pay a visit to Whitesea Island. So after lunch on the following day Sergeant Ryder equipped himself with an inch-to-the-mile map of the Blackwater area and drove out to Essex, having first found out from the local police when it would be possible to cross to the island by the causeway.

He reached the river at four o'clock. The approach was through fields by a rough track that mounted the protecting sea wall and descended on the other side. Ryder pulled up for a moment on top of the wall and surveyed the scene. He saw that he had timed his arrival well, for the causeway had only just been exposed by the falling tide. It snaked its way through drying brown mud banks and patches of weed to a shingle shore some half a mile away. Nothing was visible on the island except another high sea wall, a solitary red roof top, and a number of tall trees.

The crossing by car was less hazardous than it had looked at first sight. There were a lot of potholes, some slippery patches of mud and weed, and several sharp bends that required care. Once a car had left the hard surface, getting it back out of the mud would have been a major operation. But, at a cautious walking speed, there was no serious risk. Indeed, Ryder decided, the causeway would have been quite negotiable at night with good lights and a steady nerve.

The island itself was something of a surprise. Beyond the shingle and the wall, it had none of the rough and neglected appearance that Ryder had expected. It consisted almost entirely of well-hedged, well-kept fields of rich pasture, served by an unmetalled but entirely adequate road with a sign at the entrance—'Private. No access except on business.' Apart from one old farmhouse—the roof of which was the one Ryder had seen from the mainland—there were no more than half a dozen buildings all told. Most of them were two-story farm cottages. Only one, as far as Ryder could see, was a bungalow. In the garden of a cottage opposite, a man was digging. He was an elderly man, and he was digging in shirtsleeves a waistcoat and a cloth cap.

Ryder pulled up, got out of the car, and approached the digger. 'Good afternoon,' he said. 'Can you tell me if this is the bungalow that belongs to Mr Armitage?'

'That's right,' the man said.

'I wonder if you can help me. I understand it was occupied last week by two friends of his. A man and a woman.'

'That's right,' the man said again. He stopped digging, leaning on his fork, and looked inquiringly at Ryder.

'I'm a police officer,' Ryder told him. 'Just a routine inquiry. Nothing alarming.'

'Ah . . . Yes, a young couple, they were. Came in a little green car. Big fellow with a red beard, and a good-looking girl. Came Saturday. Left Monday morning.'

Ryder nodded. 'About what time would you say they got here?'

'Oh—near enough six o'clock.'

'Did they stay in the bungalow all the evening, do you know? Or did they go off again?'

'I did see them going off—just for a stroll around.'

'They didn't leave by car?'

'No, they didn't do that. There's nowhere to go to with a car here.'

'I wondered if they drove back to the mainland.'

The man shook his head. 'They couldn't have, Saturday night—there was a late tide. The causeway would've been covered.'

'When would it have been covered?'

'Well, now . . .' The man occupied himself for a moment with a routine tidal calculation. 'On Saturday? Around eight o'clock, I reckon.'

'I see . . . And how long would it have stayed covered?'

'Five hours,' the man said. 'Near as makes no odds.'

'So they couldn't have left the island before about one o'clock in the morning?'

'Not without wings, they couldn't. Or a boat.'

'M'm . . . Well, I'm very much obliged to you.' Ryder gave the man an affable nod, and returned to his car.

On the way back to the mainland, he stopped for a moment by the shingle shore. There were one or two small rowing boats drawn up near the bank, but none of them had oars in them. It was possible, of course, that there'd been oars at the bungalow. All the same, he found it hard to imagine the Adams couple creeping out with oars, at the risk of being observed by their neighbours opposite, and taking a boat that didn't belong to them, and rowing the half-mile of fast-running tide to start a nefarious enterprise. In any case, they'd have had no car on the mainland side, unless they'd made arrangements to leave one there beforehand. And when they returned the river would have been dry, and the boat would have been on the wrong side, and there'd have been trouble about it . . . On a reasonable balance of probabilities, it seemed to Ryder in the highest degree unlikely that Adams and his new wife had spent their wedding night driving up to Yorkshire and kidnapping Robert Quarry and murdering him. It seemed far more likely that they'd spent it in the customary way.

PART THREE

Chapter One

Burns and Ryder stayed another full day in the south, pursuing their inquiries. Burns paid another visit to Harpenden and had discreet talks with Mrs Aspinall and several other neighbours, without in any way advancing the case. Ryder worked systematically through the office files. In the afternoon both policemen conducted interviews with the office staff, alert for any helpful rumour or revealing piece of gossip. But nothing fresh emerged.

They had, as a result of their labours, gained a rather clearer view of Robert Quarry as a man—but that was about all. Their tentative interest in people with grudges had come to nothing. No suspect had been brought up in the net. All the people whose stories they'd investigated—Baird, the Bellamys, Wharton, Saxon and Adams—had had alibis or near-alibis for the night of Saturday. No hint of any additional animosities had been discovered, either in London or in Harpenden. No one had been found to suggest that Miss Johns' relationship with Quarry had been anything but friendly and correct. No trace of personal scandal had been unearthed. It had been established that almost anyone in the office might have known where Quarry was spending the weekend—but that had raised more questions than it had answered. By the time the two policemen got back to Lowark in the late evening of the third day they were tired, despondent, and still without a lead of any sort.

It had been a gruelling and unproductive trip.

From his room at headquarters, Burns reported to the Chief Constable on the fruitless journey and the bleak outlook. He proposed, he said, to see Driscoll again and try to get more information from him about Quarry's early years; and in general to continue delving into the dead man's past. It seemed the only course . . . While Burns talked, Ryder glanced through an unhelpful fingerprint report from the unit that had visited the Moor View Hotel. There had been no identifiable prints on the window ledge, not even Quarry's. Everything, everywhere, was negative . . .

Burns had just put the phone down when there was a knock at the door and Constable Williams came in. Williams was a fresh-faced young detective, not yet very experienced, but decidedly keen. The superintendent had found him reliable and likeable—but on this occasion he eyed him with less than his customary good humour. 'You've been taking your time, Constable, haven't you?'

'Sorry, sir.'

'Why the long silence?'

'Mr Watson's been away for a couple of days, sir. Up in Manchester on business. I only managed to contact him this evening.'

'All right. So what did he say?'

'He said he was absolutely sure, sir, that the whole of the dead man's arm was sticking out of the boot when he came across the car. No doubt about it at all. Right above the elbow, he said.'

'He did, did he . . .?' Burns frowned. 'What about the other hikers?'

'I couldn't find any of the others, sir.'

'Oh? Why not?'

'Well, these hikers, sir, they were all strangers to each other. They weren't a hiking club, or anything like that. They just happened to turn up together for the same hike.' Williams took a newspaper from his pocket. 'It's all here, sir. It's to do with a man who calls himself "Wanderer".'

Burns took the paper. It was a copy of the previous week's *Lowark Advertiser*. He looked at it for a moment—then reached for his bag and took out a similar copy, the one Driscoll had given him a day or two before— and passed it to Ryder. Together they studied the page that Williams had indicated.

There was a feature—a regular weekly feature, apparently—by someone using the pseudonym 'Wanderer.' Under the general heading

'Somewhere for Sunday' it gave particulars of pleasant rural hikes for people living in the Lowark area. The latest itinerary was for a walk of fifteen miles on a circular route, with a sketch map indicating each turning to be taken and arrows showing the direction of the hike. The sketch map's indicated route for that week included the track where Quarry's body had been found.

For a moment or two Burns stared at it in silent concentration. Then he looked up at Williams, all trace of gloom miraculously dissipated. 'Well, thank you, Constable. That's the most interesting bit of information we've had in this case yet. Nice work!'

Williams, looking slightly perplexed at the commendation, said 'Thank *you*, sir,' and withdrew.

Burns sat back in his chair and gently prodded tobacco into his pipe. 'Well,' he said, 'that's one little problem we don't have to worry about any more . . . And quite a dramatic shift in the case.'

Ryder was looking almost as mystified as Williams had been. I'm afraid I'm not entirely with you, sir.'

'The arm, Sergeant—the protruding arm. You know it's bothered me from the start—I never did believe the murderer could have overlooked it. Either we'd been wrongly informed about it—which, thanks to Mr Watson's positive evidence, we now know we weren't—or else the murderer had left it sticking out deliberately. That's how it seemed to me, anyway. As though he'd *wanted* it to be seen . . . But that didn't make sense—at the time. Not with the car parked out of sight of the road, on a disused track—where, except for the chance of those hikers happening along, it might not have been found for days.'

Light dawned on Ryder. 'But now we know it was almost certain to be seen.'

'Exactly. By thirty or forty "Wanderer" fans who could be relied upon to use that track on Sunday morning. The murderer had seen the local paper, and he planned it all in advance. He dumped the car at a spot he knew the hikers would pass, and to make sure they didn't just walk by it he left the arm protruding to catch their attention.'

'It's quite a notion, sir.'

'It's a lot more than a notion,' Burns said, 'and I'll tell you why. There's another bit of evidence that slots in with it—the fact that the Rover was turned round. That's been nagging away at me, too. Now I think the reason's clear. The murderer would have known from the sketch map which way the hikers would be coming, because of the arrows—and he turned the car round so that the boot and the arm would be facing them as they approached. So that they couldn't possibly miss it . . . I now feel quite sure that our murderer wanted the body to be discovered on Sunday morning, and that he took all the necessary steps to make certain it would be. What we have to decide is *why* he wanted it discovered.'

Ryder pondered. 'Sounds as though he might have been anxious to fix the time of death.'

Burns nodded. 'The longer a body's left undiscovered, the harder it is to pinpoint the moment when it became a body. You don't have to be a pathologist to know that—it stands to reason . . . So we come to the next question. Why would the murderer have wanted to fix the time of death?'

'Presumably,' Ryder said, 'because he'd worked out some sort of phoney alibi. That's the usual reason.'

'And that's what I'd say. He'd got himself organized for a death in the early hours of Sunday morning. Which brings us to the little matter of the clock that stopped at 2.31 a.m. I've always been suspicious of broken clocks and watches in murder cases. I'd now hazard a guess that the murderer smashed that clock deliberately—to reinforce the medical evidence.'

'Then the wrecked car . . .' Ryder began.

'A fake, Sergeant. If he was going to smash the clock, he had to provide some explanation. So he faked a struggle . . . And that makes sense, too. I never could see how two men struggling in such a confined space could have done all that damage. They wouldn't have had room to develop the power.'

'In which case,' Ryder said, 'we've probably been wasting our time looking out for a man with signs of injury.'

'Oh, that doesn't follow at all. He might easily have taken a few knocks before he finished Quarry off. We'll keep on looking.'

Ryder nodded. 'Anyway, we seem to have made a bit of progress, sir.'

'I think so, Sergeant. The darkest hour before the dawn, eh? We've cleared up a loose end or two—and we've confirmed some views we'd already begun to have about the murder. We know now that it was a thought-out job, not a casual affair. We know the murderer considers himself a potential suspect, or he wouldn't have bothered about an alibi plan. His constant use of gloves points the same way. Which suggests we've been on the right lines this last day or two in looking for someone with a private rather than a public motive.'

Ryder grunted. 'It would be nice if we could narrow the field a bit.'

'I think we have done,' Burns said. 'We know now that the murderer was familiar with the Lowark *Advertiser*—or at least with one issue of it. That's a new thread in the case. It doesn't help us as far as the locals are concerned, of course—but it might be a line worth following up with individuals we know about. Driscoll, for instance, might have sent copies to other people besides Quarry. Quarry might have shown his copy to a friend or a neighbour—someone like Aspinall, for instance. The new company chairman, Baird, might well have seen it—and shown it to others. So might Miss Johns . . . And, of course, there's "Wanderer" himself. He'd have had the best of opportunities to use the track for a murder alibi—and we've no idea who *he is*. We'd better check on him first thing in the morning.'

Chapter Two

At home that evening, Burns was able to relax a little for the first time in days. There was no sign yet of a real break in the case—but at least over the 'Wanderer' discovery he'd been able to use his professional talents to some degree . . . Anyhow, it felt good to have his jacket off and his slippers on and Alice to chat to.

Over a late pot of tea and an omelette, he brought her up to date about his activities. He rarely confided the details of his cases to her, but she liked to be kept broadly in the picture, and he liked it too. That way his work was a bridge between them instead of a gap—and sometimes she made quite helpful comments. To-day, though, her chief interest was unashamedly personal.

'I suppose there isn't any chance you'll finish it off before Tuesday, is there?' she asked.

Burns shook his head. 'Very little, I'm afraid, on present showing.'

'Who do you think will take over from you, dear?'

'I don't know . . . Bryant or Ellis, I suppose. That'll be up to Ivison.'

'Has he said any more about it?'

'No.'

'Have you?'

'Not yet, I've still got a few more days.'

'Well, as long as he's keeping it in mind . . . I bought a book to-day, Joe—I saw it in Smith's and I couldn't resist it. It gives a complete list of French camp sites, with all the details about them and some wonderful pictures. There are two sites actually on the banks of the River Dordogne—you could practically fish from the van window!'

'That would be something new,' Burns said, with a chuckle. 'Anyway, I'm all for river banks. You must show me the book after supper.'

'There's a bit in it about the weather, too. Apparently it can be marvellous in the Dordogne in early November. They get hardly any rain, and lots of sun.'

Burns gave a little sigh. 'I'm certainly looking forward to it.' He moved his empty plate aside and finished his tea and started to dismantle his space pipe. 'If only I could get this case cleared up . . . What I need is one good suspect—someone I could work on. Things could move quickly then . . . It's the routine slogging that takes so long—the interviews, the journeys . . . Especially the journeys. I'm beginning to feel I know Harpenden almost as well as Lowark.'

'Yes—you've been there three times, haven't you?' Alice sat for a moment in reflective silence. 'That Mrs Quarry must be a strange sort of girl, Joe.'

'Why do you say that?'

'Well, not knowing anything about her husband's affairs. Not even about him quarrelling with that stockbroker man, for instance. I'd have thought she'd have been interested in what went on, if she was as fond of him as she was supposed to be.'

'Perhaps he didn't want to tell her.'

'No, perhaps he didn't . . . It wouldn't suit me, I know that. I'd find it very dull if you just ate and slept here, and we never talked about what you were doing.'

'But *my* job's to do with people, dear. Quarry's was business money. I don't suppose even you would be interested in stocks and shares and investments.'

'Chance would be a fine thing!' said Alice.

Chapter Three

As it happened, Burns and Ryder converged on headquarters at the same moment the next day, and went into the building together. Burns had already planned the morning's activities. Constable Williams was to man the office. Ryder was to check up on 'Wanderer'. He himself would have another talk with Driscoll. Then the three of them would meet and review the situation . . . But in minutes after he and Ryder had entered the office, they were faced with an entirely new development.

On Burns' desk there was a letter which had come by the morning delivery, and which had been opened by Constable Williams. The envelope was addressed, in rough capitals scrawled by a ball point pen, to POLICE STATION LOWARK: and it was postmarked 'Lowark, 6 p.m.' In the top left-hand corner of the envelope were the words QUARRY MURDER. Inside was a single sheet of paper with the unsigned message: QUARRY WAS HAVING AN AFFAIR WITH MRS DRISCOLL.

Burns, handling the letter by the tip of a corner, passed it to Ryder, who read it. For a moment, as they digested the message, neither of them made any comment. They were both very accustomed to anonymous letters. Nine times out of ten the communications were worthless. Once in a while they could suggest a useful lead. They could never be ignored.

Burns spoke first. 'What do you make of it, Sergeant?'

'Well, sir,' Ryder said, 'as I see it, the implication is that Driscoll murdered Quarry because he discovered that Quarry was having an affair with his wife.'

Burns gazed benignly at his sergeant. 'Yes—I think we might say that that was what was intended. Otherwise the writer would hardly have put QUARRY MURDER – on the envelope!'

'He could be a nut case, of course.'

'He could, indeed.'

'If he isn't, he's either making a false charge or he's found out about an actual affair and is telling the truth.'

'Why would he make a false charge—assuming that he's sane?'

'Well, he might have had it in for Driscoll and/or Mrs Driscoll—for some reason . . . Or maybe he is telling the truth. We know Quarry was a fairly frequent daytime visitor at the Driscoll home—and often on his own. We know Betty Driscoll rather admired him. He could have made use of his opportunities. And Driscoll could have got wind of what was happening. Then he'd have had quite a motive. The letter fills a big gap in the case against Driscoll that we were discussing earlier.'

'It leaves other big gaps unfilled,' Burns said. 'Like Driscoll going out of his way to tell me he knew Quarry's room number. And the problem of how he'd have returned to Yorkshire without a car . . . Let's get back to the letter. Are there any other possibilities that strike you?'

'I suppose someone could have wanted us to go off on a new scent, sir.'

'The murderer, you mean?'

'Could be.'

'M'm . . . The same thought occurred to me. But I don't know why he should want us to go off on a new scent when we're not on a scent at all. He's in no danger—unfortunately.'

'He may mink he is, sir. We've asked a lot of people a lot of questions. Perhaps we've been warmer than we realized.'

'I wish I could believe that.' Burns broke off as the telephone rang. Ryder picked up the instrument beside him. 'Yes . . .? Speaking . . . Oh, yes . . .?' The sergeant indicated the extension beside Burns. Burns raised the receiver gently, and listened. The speaker was the manager of the Fleetway Cars garage in York.

'I thought I'd better ring you, Sergeant,' the manager was saying.

'It's about that Rover speedometer reading you asked about Robert Quarry's Rover. Quite unintentionally, I'm afraid we misled you.'

'Oh?'

'Yes. You'll remember the man in charge of the service was away delivering a car the day you called? Jock Paton—he was delivering a Jag. Well, when he got back we talked about the Rover and Robert Quarry, and I mentioned the mileage point to him—and he said young Terry *hadn't* made a mistake. He said he and another mechanic were looking over the car when Terry wasn't there—admiring the model and the fine shape it was in and so on—and they both looked at the speedo to see what the car had done, and the mileage was definitely 36,501, not 36,301. Jock's absolutely certain about it, and so is the other man. No question about it at all. I don't suppose it's important, but I thought you ought to know.'

'Yes, indeed,' Ryder said. 'Thanks a lot . . . We're very much obliged to you.'

Chapter Four

There was a moment of silence, a meeting of puzzled eyes, as the two men hung up.

Then Burns said, 'There could be something wrong with the speedometer, I suppose. We'd better have it checked right away.'

Ryder shook his head. 'I had it checked, sir—when that first discrepancy came to light. PC Granger had it out and gave it a thorough testing. It was working perfectly. Instrument, cable, everything . . .'

'Oh . . . Well, in that case, we appear to have a distinctly intriguing situation on our hands.'

'Yes, sir . . .' Ryder was jotting down some figures which were now firmly in his memory. 'If the mileage at the time of service was 36,501, and the car did at least 107 miles after that—12 to the hotel and 95 to Lowark, as we know it did—then the speedometer should now read at least 36,608. In fact it reads 36,459—149 miles less.'

'Which, as Euclid used to say, is absurd.'

'Quite impossible, sir. Unless somebody wound back the speedometer.'

'Obviously somebody *did* wind it back,' Burns said. 'There can't be any other explanation. Now let's see . . . Quarry collected the car from the garage around midday. Presumably he lunched somewhere—we don't know where, but the chances are the car would either have been under his own eye or else parked in too public a place for tampering. Then he was out on the moors with it in the afternoon, and back at the hotel with it in the late afternoon, when he made those phone calls . . . Not much opportunity for anyone to interfere with it in that time, would you say?'

'I'd say none at all, sir.'

'And between tea and dinner, when the car was parked in the drive, guests would have been coming back from outings, strolling in the grounds and so on. Nothing could have been done then.'

'Not a chance.'

'How about after dark?'

'I doubt if the job could have been done after dark, sir—not out of doors. I was watching Granger at work—it's a fiddly business, with some tiny screws to get out. You need a really good fight . . . Were you thinking the murderer might have done it, later in the night?'

'I was wondering.'

'I'd say it's unlikely. *Most unlikely*'.

Burns nodded slowly. 'I'm inclined to agree with you—and for a different reason. Winding a speedometer back seems to me to have more than an accidental connection with taking a car in to be serviced by a strange garage when the service isn't urgently necessary and you're supposed to be having a restful holiday. The service establishes a certain mileage—and then you cook the figures! See what I mean?'

'I certainly do, sir.'

'All of which leaves us with only one answer—that Quarry did it himself . . . Have you any idea how long it takes to wind back a speedo, Sergeant?'

'Well,' Ryder said, 'it took Granger about fifteen minutes to dismantle the instrument when he was checking—and about the same time to refit it. 'Winding the figures back would be a simple job once it was off—say another ten minutes. For a man who knew what he was doing, I'd guess an overall time of forty-five minutes would be about right.'

'And Quarry *would* have known what he was doing.'

'Very much so—he was a technical man. I believe his Lowark factory actually makes speedometers.'

'So he could easily have done the job while he was up on the moors on Saturday afternoon.'

'Easily. Without any risk of being disturbed.'

'Right—then I think we've got to assume he did it . . . So now we come to the next point. *Why* would Quarry have wanted to wind his speedo back? What would he have stood to gain by it?'

Ryder reflected. 'Well,' he said at last, 'he'd hardly have been aiming to make an extra quid or two when he eventually flogged the car! It sounds to me as though he was trying to conceal a journey.'

'Yes . . . But not a journey he'd already made. In that case there'd have been no point in establishing the mileage at service.'

'A journey he was planning to make, then.'

Burns nodded. 'That's about it . . . Sergeant, this is where our case takes a very dramatic turn. We've been assuming all along that Quarry was abducted from his hotel, because that was what the evidence seemed to indicate. Now it begins to look as though he left voluntarily. On a secret journey planned beforehand for the Saturday night, which he hoped to cover up by fiddling the speedo. Out to somewhere, and back to the hotel in time for his date with Driscoll in the morning. A journey he never completed, because he was killed.'

'Which would account for the shortfall in mileage.'

'Exactly. He didn't foresee his fate, he thought he'd return, and he wound the speedo back too far.'

'It figures,' Ryder said.

'So do a lot of other things, Sergeant—now we're thinking in terms of a planned secret departure. The great lengths he went to to cover up his intentions—which naturally took everybody in. Booking at the hotel for two nights, writing and phoning his wife about his plans, fixing up to meet Driscoll, giving the impression he was a relaxed and cheerful guest with nothing on his mind . . .'

'Ordering whisky,' Ryder said, 'so he could be seen in bed—before he got up and dressed again.'

Burns nodded. 'And it's clear now why he made that rather surprising choice of a hotel. He'd been there before—he knew it was just the place for a quiet getaway by night. Ground floor annexe—with a view, to explain why he chose it. Low window to climb out of, car park facilities well down the drive, drive sloping to the road. I can see why he wasn't deterred by the poor food!'

'Yes,' Ryder said. 'It was all very well thought out. Brilliant, really. If he hadn't run into trouble and got killed, he'd have covered up his journey completely. With all those signs of his intentions, and the speedo showing no extra mileage, the evidence that he'd been in the hotel all night would have been overwhelming . . . I wonder what the heck he had in mind?'

'Well—that's our next problem.' There was a little pause. Then Burns said, 'Of course, Sergeant, you realize what all this adds up to . . .? It's the only case I've ever known where a murderer and his victim both felt in need of an alibi on the same night. I'd say it's unique.'

Chapter Five

They broke off the discussion at that point while Burns attended to more pressing matters. First, he called in Constable Williams and dispatched him to the office of the *Lowark Advertiser* on the trail of 'Wanderer'. Then he became immersed in a long telephone conversation with the Chief Constable about the new developments.

Ryder went up to the canteen for coffee and a cigarette.

He sat in a corner on his own, doodling on a piece of paper, and thinking about Quarry slipping away in the night on a secret expedition that had led to his death. Thinking about the track at Lowark and how he'd come to be there. Thinking about the anonymous letter, and the Driscolls . . . Presently he stopped doodling and started figuring again.

He was still alone, and sunk in thought, when the superintendent joined him with a cup of coffee. 'Well,' Burns said, glancing at the paper, 'have you worked out all the answers?'

'No, sir—but I've got an idea.'

'About what Quarry was up to?'

'And about what happened to him. But it is only an idea.'

'Let's have it,' Burns said, 'We shan't get anywhere by just sitting and looking at mileages, shall we?'

'Well, it goes back to the letter we had, sir—and John Driscoll. It seems to me that he's still very much in the picture. The case against him is different now, with all this new information—but I think it's stronger.'

'Go right ahead, Sergeant. I agree the situation's changed—and any theory's better than none.'

'Well, sir,' Ryder said, with the familiar glint in his eye, 'my idea is that Quarry *was* having an affair with Betty Driscoll, as the letter says. But with Driscoll around in Lowark most of the time, he didn't have much chance to meet her alone. Then last week he got this phone call from Driscoll with the suggestion about shuffling Sullivan off to some other factory—and he saw his opportunity. He'd go north to discuss the suggestion, and he'd make it the excuse to send Driscoll off on a trip. He knew he could do that, because he was Driscoll's boss. With Driscoll out of the way for a couple of days, he'd be able to fix something up with Betty. Which was why, on this occasion, he didn't take his wife up with him.'

'I'm with you so far,' Burns said.

'Well, the plan went smoothly. Driscoll cleared off on his round of the factories. Quarry put up at the Moor View. On Saturday afternoon he phoned Betty—ostensibly to find out where Driscoll was, so he could contact him about the shoot. But he also made an arrangement to meet Betty somewhere on the Saturday evening—I'm assuming they were already on such close terms that he knew she'd fall in with any suggestion—all he had to do was fix the time and place. And because he was sure about her, he'd already planned his alibi precautions—the speedo change and the hotel deception—just as a safeguard in case anyone later suspected the meeting had taken place.'

'M'm . . . Where do you suggest this tryst would have been held?'

Ryder referred to his piece of paper. 'This is where I'm in a spot of trouble, sir—over the mileage. You'll remember we had 149 miles unaccounted for—miles we reckoned Quarry would have expected to do if he'd lived. Well, 95 of those would have been for his return to the hotel—which leaves 54 unexplained. So I'm suggesting that he planned to meet Betty something like 27 miles beyond Lowark.'

'Why would he have done that?'

'Maybe because he and Betty knew some specially quiet place around there where they'd met before. Obviously they wouldn't have wanted to meet close to Lowark, where they were both well known. And Betty had her own car—it would have been quite an easy trip for her.'

'I see . . . Go on.'

'Well, now we come to Driscoll. My idea is that he suspected the liaison. And that Quarry guessed he suspected, which was why he took such precautions. Anyway, instead of going to his cottage on Saturday night, Driscoll kept watch at the hotel, and when he saw Quarry sneaking out of his window at midnight or thereabouts, he decided his suspicions were right. He followed him, and on some quiet stretch of road near Lowark he passed and stopped him and—maybe after a row—killed him. He didn't do it earlier, because he'd already got a plan in mind to knock him off near Lowark—to suggest a factory motive . . . He then drove the Rover to the track—having done his homework on 'Wanderer' beforehand—and set the scene to his satisfaction. Broken clock, wrecked interior, arm out, car turned round—all that stuff. Then he returned to his own car and drove back to his cottage in time to be at the hotel at nine o'clock as though nothing had happened.'

Burns grunted. 'You're a fast talker, Sergeant—slow down a little, will you . . .? Why would Driscoll have wanted to set any scene? It wouldn't have mattered to him when the body was discovered and whether the time of death was fixed. He didn't have an alibi for that night anyway.'

'I know, sir. That's why he arranged things the way he did. He decided the next best thing to having a good alibi was *not* having one—and making it appear that the actual murderer had one. A sort of double bluff.'

'Oh—very ingenious,' Burns said. 'Very subtle. It might even work . . . But do you really suppose Driscoll would have thought of that?'

'I thought of it, sir. Why shouldn't he?'

'A fair question.' Burns was silent for a moment. 'The trouble is, Sergeant, your theory doesn't stand up in other ways . . . In the first place, the only evidence we have for this liaison between Quarry and Betty Driscoll is the anonymous letter—and, frankly, I don't believe a word of it. Not just because Driscoll and his wife seemed to have a good relationship with each other—I know one can easily be misled about such things—but because everything we know indicates that Quarry was completely sold on Alma—and for very good reasons. She's an outstandingly attractive girl, and he'd been married to her for less than a year. Why should he wander? He certainly showed no sign of doing so—in fact it's only a few months ago that he willed almost the whole of his fortune to her—and she'd have got even more if he'd lived long enough to make a new will and cut out his niece. Surely that's not the behaviour of a man on the prowl for another woman?'

'Sounds pretty dotty, sir, I admit.'

'Then again,' Burns went on, 'your theory overlooks a most important fact—that Quarry's main alibi arrangement, the car service, was on Saturday morning, and that there's no evidence that he knew *then* that Driscoll proposed to spend Saturday night alone at his cottage, and so would be out of the way. For all Quarry knew when he took that car in, Driscoll might have intended to go home to Lowark for the night. The service and the speedometer change would have been the wildest speculation on Quarry's part.'

'True,' Ryder said.

'And there's another point, Sergeant—the most important one of all, in my view. Would Quarry really have gone to such vast trouble to conceal a journey, merely on account of an assignation he'd made with a woman which probably wouldn't be discovered anyway? Would any man? I just don't believe it.'

'You think he had a more important reason, sir?'

'I'm sure he had. I'm sure he'd never have organized such an elaborate scheme otherwise. If he needed an alibi that badly, it suggests to me that he was planning to do something that would almost certainly be discovered afterwards, something that could point to him, something that without an alibi might well be brought home to him. Something really serious—something criminal.'

'You mean—like a killing, sir?'

'That's exactly what I mean,' Burns said.

Chapter Six

There was a reflective pause, as the ripples of Burns's pebble spread. Then Ryder said, 'Well, we know of several people who might have wanted to get rid of Quarry. Do we know of anyone *he* might have wanted to get rid of?'

'I certainly don't,' Burns said. 'Not at the moment.'

'How about Sullivan?' Ryder suggested. 'In the hope of ending the strike . . . Could Quarry have arranged a secret meeting with him, intending to kill him? And then got killed himself? A murder attempt that backfired?'

Burns shook his head. 'It's a pretty far-fetched idea, Sergeant, isn't it? Killing Sullivan wouldn't necessarily have stopped the strike. It might well have made things worse. Quarry would have known that—he wasn't a stupid man. Far from it. No, I'm sure we've got to look for a stronger motive than that. Much stronger. And a much more personal one . . .'

'It's hard to imagine Quarry with any strong motive for killing,' Ryder said. 'A rich man, secure in a big job, no unsatisfied ambitions, not hating anyone's guts as far as we know, married to a smashing wife and very happy about it—if we don't take the anonymous letter seriously. A very lucky chap, I'd have said.'

'That's certainly how it seems on the surface,' Burns agreed. 'So it's difficult to know where to start. Yet there must be something—something we don't know about. Something we haven't dug up yet. Some secret. There must be . . .'

'How about a spot of blackmail, sir?'

'Blackmail? By him, you mean?'

'No—*of* him . . . It's the sort of thing that does happen to rich men.'

'Well, it's an interesting idea,' Burns said. 'Would you care to develop it?'

'I don't mind having a go, sir.' Ryder allowed himself a few moments of thought—then embarked on a story with an air of unshakable confidence. 'Let's say Quarry *was* being blackmailed. About something unsavoury in his past. By someone who lives, say, twenty or thirty miles beyond Lowark—just to take care of the mileage problem. Someone he's known to have a business or personal relationship with—so there's a connection between them. Maybe someone who works at the factory. And this blackmailer instructs Quarry to meet him near his home on Saturday night and hand over some cash . . .'

'Yes?' Burns said, encouragingly.

'Well,' Ryder continued, 'Quarry has decided to kill this blackmailer and get him off his back. But because of the known connection between them—maybe some public row they've had—he thinks he may be suspected of the killing. Or at least questioned about it. And naturally he wants to be quite sure he'll be in the clear. So he fixes up his weekend alibi, with the speedo turned back to cover the double journey and a good line of talk about staying in the hotel. Then he meets the blackmailer as arranged. Around 2.30 a.m. he attacks the man with some blunt instrument he's brought with him. But things go wrong, and in the fight that develops it's actually the blackmailer who kills Quarry. Not with intent—more in panicky self-defence. Now the blackmailer has a body on his hands—a body that can get him in deep trouble unless he can provide some alternative explanation for the death—like a factory motive. So he drives it to Lowark in the Rover and dumps it at the track. Then he makes his way back to his own car, and pushes off home.'

'M'm . . . Well, it's a good try, Sergeant. But you seem to be up against the same problem with your blackmailer as you were with Driscoll. If the blackmailer hadn't planned any killing, he wouldn't have had an alibi for that night. So why all the arrangements at the track?'

'The same reason I gave for Driscoll, sir. The double bluff.'

'I see. He was clever, too.'

'He must have been. Blackmailers often are.'

'But whereas Driscoll would have had time to plan the double bluff in advance,' Burns said, 'this man wouldn't. According to your theory he was taken by surprise—so he wouldn't have had time to plan anything. And I doubt if he'd have had the clarity of mind, either. I can't see anyone working out a complicated scheme like that, more or less off the cuff, when he'd just unintentionally committed a murder. He'd have been in far too much of a flap.'

'I don't know about that, sir. If the murder had happened at 2.30 a.m., he'd have had plenty of time to work things out. Time to cool off and make plans—especially if he was familiar with the ground. I see him as a man with local knowledge of Lowark, a man who would have known about 'Wanderer' and the track and the hikers. If he'd had all that knowledge at his fingertips, the idea could have come to him quite quickly.'

'What about logistics, Sergeant? If he drove the Rover to the track from a rendezvous point twenty or thirty miles away, how did he get back to his car in the middle of the night?'

Ryder shrugged. 'He could have got a hitch, I suppose. Told some story. At a pinch he could even have walked a good part of the way. In his position, I'm sure I'd have managed to get back somehow.'

'What about the car mileage problem? If Quarry actually kept an appointment at a place he'd agreed on and foreseen, and the Rover was then driven back to Lowark by the blackmailer, the speedometer would have shown the full journey both ways, and there'd have been no shortfall in the mileage apart from the 95 miles to the hotel that wasn't done.'

'Yes, that presents a difficulty,' Ryder admitted—but without any loss of composure. 'I suppose, sir, there could have been a last-minute change in the rendezvous—after Quarry had made the speedo alteration. He could have rung the blackmailer before he returned to the hotel on Saturday afternoon—to confirm the appointment, say—and been given new instructions. Told of a meeting place quite close to Lowark, instead of twenty or thirty miles beyond it. That could have accounted for the shortfall—and Quarry could have decided the difference in mileage wasn't enough for him to worry about . . . As it happens, a move like that would also dispose of the logistics problem. The blackmailer's car could have been left somewhere quite close to the track, and he'd have had no difficulty in getting away.'

'You twist and turn a bit, Sergeant, don't you?'

Ryder grinned. 'I'm only trying to make the facts fit the theory, sir.'

'You certainly are! Anyway, leaving these movement details aside, I can't help thinking it would be a very rash blackmailer who'd suggest meeting a tough man like Quarry alone in a quiet spot in the middle of the night. Rather asking for trouble, wouldn't you say?'

'That would depend on the blackmailer, sir. Quarry was tough, but there are plenty of bigger, stronger men around—blokes that reckon they can look after themselves in any situation. We know a few who'd take a chance like that for a large packet of dough.'

'Well, you may be right about that. But can you really see Quarry as a man who'd ever have allowed himself to be blackmailed? This is a man, don't forget, who had stood up to a strike for six weeks, even though it was ruining his firm—stood up to it practically single-handed, and against all the pressures. An ex-commando, too. Wasn't he just the sort of man who'd tell a blackmailer to go to hell—and damn the consequences?'

'If the position was serious enough,' Ryder said, 'I reckon any man would go along with a blackmailer for a while. Suppose, for the sake of argument, Quarry had had some kind of homosexual relationship with someone before his marriage. After all, he did reach middle age before marrying—its not beyond the bounds of possibility. Then he was suddenly threatened with exposure by this guy—exposure to the new wife he was nuts about. Even Quarry, in that position, might have paid—once or twice—for temporary silence, while he worked out a foolproof murder plan.'

Burns was silent for quite a while. Finally he said, 'You know, Sergeant, I'm impressed by that little speech ... Your particular blackmailer is just a figment, of course—and I think your particular theory is as full of holes as a sieve. But blackmail in general—blackmail as a murder motive for Quarry—that's another matter. There *could* have been something Quarry wanted hushed up—something he was prepared to pay someone, for a while, to keep quiet about.'

'I just thought it was a possible line of inquiry, sir.'

'It also happens to be the only one we have ... I'm inclined to think we should pursue it.'

'What do we do, then, sir?'

'A bit more delving, I should think. If Quarry was being blackmailed, and if he paid out any large sum, it should show up somewhere—in his financial affairs, his bank account. We could find out if he'd withdrawn any large sums in cash lately. Anyway, financial transactions are often illuminating—and we're certainly in need of light. Let's take another trip down south tomorrow ...'

Chapter Seven

With no more new material to work on, and a heavy programme of investigation ahead, Burns decided to leave the office early that day and take a rest. After holding an informal press conference in the afternoon, he went off home to think aloud about the latest developments, with Alice as sounding board. Ryder stayed behind to polish off a few routine jobs—including getting the anonymous letter off to Forensic for tests that no one expected would prove very helpful. Also, at Burns' suggestion, to send a set of Quarry's own fingerprints to be checked at the Criminal Record Office. If the dead man had by any chance been blackmailable, there was always the possibility that he might have had a police record at some time.

The sergeant was on the point of leaving himself when Constable Williams came. 'Evening, Sarge,' he said cheerfully. His expression indicated that he had some news he was dying to impart. 'Has the Chief gone?'

Ryder nodded. 'An hour ago. Did you get the low-down on "Wanderer"?'

'I sure did,' Williams said. 'You'll be surprised when I tell you.'

'After what's been happening today, nothing could surprise me. What's the gen on him?'

Well, to start with, he's a she.'

'Go on!'

'It's a fact. A spinster lady named McKay. Daughter of a clergyman, Lowark born and bred, sixty-three next birthday and still going strong.'

'You mean an old girl of sixty-three hikes fifteen miles every week for an article?'

'No, Sarge, she rides a bike.'

Ryder grinned. 'The crafty old hen!'

'The editor sent a special message—if possible would we keep the information confidential. He doesn't want his readers to know.'

'I'll bet he doesn't,' Ryder said. 'Well—I guess that takes care of "Wanderer"!'

PART FOUR

Chapter One

The manager of the Harpenden branch of the National Central Bank said, 'Everything's ready for you, gentlemen. Mrs Quarry's given her permission, and Head Office say they've no objection in the special circumstances. This way, please.'

Burns and Ryder followed him into a small office. The time was almost three o'clock in the afternoon—much later than Burns had intended when he'd planned his day. But the morning had been busy. First, there'd been Forensic on the blower about the anonymous letter—no prints, as foreseen; gloves almost certainly used; no help from envelope, stamp or ink . . . Then Ivison had rung for the latest situation report . . . Then Burns had had his own phoning to do. A call to Miss Johns, to find out where Quarry had kept his personal account. Before his marriage, it seemed, when he'd had the flat in St John's Wood, he'd banked at a local branch there; since moving to the country he'd naturally switched. A call, then, to Harpenden, to ask for the bank's co-operation. After that there'd been the two-and-a-half-hour drive. Normally the superintendent would have been philosophical about the slow progress of the case; you couldn't rush an open-field inquiry. But with his eye constantly on a ringed date on the calendar, any delay irked him.

The manager had set out all the material on the table. A modest pile of paid cheques going back just under a year; paying-in slips; current account statements; deposit account statements; and a little correspondence with the bank . . . Burns divided up the pile, and the two policemen settled down to a thorough investigation of Quarry's recent financial transactions.

The search, from the beginning, proved a disappointment, for the cheques related almost entirely to the Quarrys' domestic economy. There were regular housekeeping cheques to Alma; payment for rates, electricity and fuel; payments to garages and local clubs and wine merchants and repair men—the normal outgoings of a solid citizen. But there were no large items at all—let alone the substantial withdrawals of cash that might have supported a blackmail theory. Everything that had passed in and out of this account was chicken feed. The current balance had rarely exceeded a thousand pounds, and the deposit balance hardly more than fifteen hundred.

Finally, Burns sought out the manager. 'I'm completely at a loss,' he said. 'I can't understand how anyone, as well-to-do as Quarry could have had such modest sums in his bank account.'

The manager smiled. 'A shrewd man like Mr Quarry didn't keep large sums lying idle, Superintendent. He made his money work for him—like all rich men. I'm quite sure he was fully invested.'

'Why do none of these cheques relate to any investments?'

'Oh, he had another account—possibly several. I believe his main business was conducted through the City and General in Cornhill. He only used this bank for his local requirements.'

Burns could have kicked himself. And Miss Johns, too, who hadn't asked *which* bank, or mentioned the City and General. But of course he had said Quarry's personal account—so Miss Johns could hardly be blamed. He looked at his watch. With chagrin he saw that it was too late now to approach the City and General that day. Time was running out, and he'd wasted a whole afternoon.

Ryder said, 'I wouldn't let it worry you, sir—really I wouldn't. You'll be basking in the sun in a week's time. What will it matter then?'

'Well, you know how it is, Sergeant. You get all keyed up, living with a case day and night, thinking of nothing else . . . The only way you can get free from the thing is to find the answer.'

The two men were having a beer at the bar of the Belsize Park motel where they'd put up for the night. Both were inwardly chafing at the enforced hold-up. They couldn't even pass the evening in useful discussion, since they'd covered all the ground. Without more facts, there was nothing new to discuss.

It was Ryder, brooding over the situation and his beer, who finally came up with a suggestion.

'I was thinking, sir,' he said. 'If there's anything at all in this blackmail notion, there'd have had to be a pretty large sum of money involved, wouldn't there? I mean, if the thing Quarry wanted hushed up was only worth a trivial sum, he'd hardly have been seriously concerned. If he was prepared to kill on account of it, it must have been worth something really big to him. Maybe thousands . . .'

'I should think that's very possible,' Burns said.

'And if Quarry was fully invested, like the bank manager told us, he might have had to sell something quite substantial. Some of his investments.'

'Well?'

'So why don't we look up that broker who handled Quarry's affairs till recently—Peter Saxon? We've got his address—and he might be able to help us.'

Burns seized eagerly on the suggestion. 'That's a splendid idea. Give him a ring, Sergeant, and see if he's in.'

Ryder departed. In a few minutes he was back, looking much more cheerful. 'He'll see us after dinner, sir. Eight-thirty at his home.'

'Excellent,' Burns said. 'You never know—he might have just the gen we need.'

They arrived at the top of the old Victorian house just as Saxon was putting out an empty milk bottle. 'Bachelor chores,' he said with a grimace. 'The price of freedom! Come in, gentlemen.'

They went in. Burns introduced the sergeant. Saxon found them chairs and offered them a drink, which they declined.

'Well, what is it this time, Superintendent? I'm not still under suspicion, I hope?'

Burns smiled. 'Not in the least, Mr Saxon. It's a small matter of information, that's all. We're interested to know whether Robert Quarry made any large sales of securities during recent months—sales that weren't followed by comparable purchases. As his former broker, perhaps you could help us.'

'What do you call a *large* sale?' Saxon asked.

'That's a little difficult . . . Shall we say, as a sort of indication, something in the region of ten thousand pounds or more? Preferably effected on a single day, or over a very short period of time.'

Saxon shook his head. 'There was nothing like that while I was handling his portfolio. I did suggest a few small changes from time to time—not always with very happy results, as you know—but nothing of that order. Naturally I can't tell you what happened after he left us.'

'M'm . . .' Burns looked disappointed. 'Do you know who his new brokers were?'

'I believe he went to Webb and Miller. They're at London Wall—you'll find them in the book. But I must say I'd be very surprised indeed if he'd sold heavily in the past month or two. In fact, I think I'd have heard about it.'

'You mean it would have caused comment?'

'It'd have been all over Throgmorton Street, if he'd sold substantially in the present state of the market. There'd soon have been gossip about the liquidity of his company.'

'Why do you say "in the present state of the market"?'

'Well, we're just coming to the end of a very long bear market. Share prices have been falling steadily for two or three years, and now they're bumping along the bottom. No investor in his senses would sell at this stage, unless he was forced to. Everyone's locked in, waiting for things to improve . . . Which is why I think I'd have heard if Quarry had sold heavily. He'd have been a startling exception to the rule—and we'd all have wanted to know the reason.'

'Yes, I see . . . Well, you make it sound pretty definite. I don't think we need trouble you any more.' Burns looked across at Ryder and got to his feet. 'I'm very grateful to you, Mr Saxon, for your expert advice.'

'A pleasure, Superintendent. There'll be no commission this time.'

Burns gave a fleeting smile. 'If the market's so bad, I imagine you brokers must be feeling the draught a bit?'

'You can say that again! There won't be many bonuses this Christmas, I can tell you. Still, it's all part of the game.'

They went into the hall. Saxon held out his hand. 'Goodbye, Superintendent.'

'Goodbye, Mr Saxon.' Burns grasped the hand firmly. Saxon winced a little—then worked his fingers, as though easing them. Burns, looking at the hand in surprise, saw that the knuckle of the middle finger was slightly enlarged. 'I'm sorry . . .' he began.

'Not at all, Superintendent. My fault entirely. I'm always forgetting the damned thing.'

'What's the trouble—rheumatism?'

'No—I did it playing squash, back in July. Banged it against a wall and cracked a bone. It healed long ago, but I still get the odd twinge. Quite trivial, really.'

'These trivial things can be a great nuisance,' Burns said. 'I've had some. All that waiting about in hospital queues, eh?'

Saxon laughed. 'The old Welfare State? Not for me, I'm afraid. I've got a friendly private doctor a couple of doors away—he fixed everything. Well, goodbye again. Goodbye, Sergeant.'

Ryder held the car door open. Burns stood on the pavement beside it, frowning. 'I *wonder* . . .'

'He said it happened in July, sir—and that's what it looks like. No bruising, nothing much to see. Is there any reason to disbelieve him?'

'None whatever, Sergeant.'

'And you did confirm his alibi, sir.'

'I know . . . But it is the first case of injury we've come across—and we have been looking for one . . .' Burns hesitated. 'I think I'll try to check. Hold on, I won't be long.'

He walked to the left for fifty yards, pausing at two small blocks of converted flats that showed the names of the tenants by the front doors. There was no indication of a doctor among them. He walked back past the car. There was another block of flats that yielded nothing, then an old-fashioned detached house. A brass plate at the gate of the house said 'A.S. Hutchins, M.D.' Burns went up the path and rang the bell. A woman opened the door.

'Is the doctor at home?' Burns asked, raising his bowler.

The woman inspected him. 'It's not his surgery time. Is it urgent?'

'I'm a police officer,' Burns said. 'I'd be obliged if Dr Hutchins could spare me a few moments.'

'Oh . . . Well, come in, please.' The woman showed Burns into a comfortable waiting-room, and disappeared.

In a few minutes, she returned. 'Will you come into the surgery?' Burns followed her. The doctor was rising from his desk. He was dapper, fiftyish, alert, and—when he spoke—pleasantly Scottish. 'Good evening, Officer,' he said. 'What's the trouble?'

Burns introduced himself and showed his warrant card. 'I won't keep you long, Doctor. I'd like to ask you a question about a patient of yours.'

'Very well, Superintendent. Though I shan't necessarily answer it. Who's the patient?'

'A man named Peter Saxon. He lives just along the road from you.'

'Ah, yes.'

'I've just come from his flat. He tells me he injured a finger last July, and that you treated it. I've absolutely no reason to doubt what he says. All I want is confirmation.'

'Well—that seems pretty harmless.' Hutchins went to a cabinet, flipped through some cards, and drew one out. 'Here we are. July 8th. Middle finger of right hand. X-rayed July 9th. Cracked bone . . . Is that what you wanted?'

Burns gave a resigned smile. 'Thank you, Doctor— that's what I expected. I'm sorry to have bothered you.'

Hutchins accompanied him to the front door. 'The finger's not troubling him, is it?'

'Not seriously. I gripped his hand rather hard when I said goodbye.'

'M'm . . . He shouldn't be feeling anything now. Perhaps he stopped using ball too soon.'

'His ball?'

'Physiotherapy. I told him to get a small rubber ball and keep on squeezing it. It's the best exercise I know for getting a damaged finger-joint back to normal.'

Ryder said, 'I don't believe it, sir. I just don't believe we could be that lucky.'

'Of course you don't, Sergeant. Neither do I. It's altogether too much to hope for ... But the fact is, we've never explained the presence of that ball. That unusually small ball ... And Saxon did have a professional connection with Quarry. So we've got to make sure.'

'We'll need his prints,' Ryder said.

'I know.'

'Which will put him on his guard—if he's got anything to guard against.'

'Not necessarily.' Burns took his murder bag from the back of the car. 'It's the old dog that knows the best tricks.' He walked quickly away and disappeared into the block where Saxon lived.

Almost at once, he was back. Ryder said, 'Forgotten something, sir?'

'Forgotten something, Sergeant? Certainly not.'

'But the prints ...?'

'I've got them.'

Ryder stared at him. 'But you were only gone about sixty seconds.'

Burns opened his bag and passed something to Ryder. 'Handle with care, Sergeant.'

Ryder removed the cloth from the object. It was an empty milk bottle.

The time was after midnight. Back at the Lowark headquarters, two police experts summoned from their homes by telephone were hard at work. On a rubber ball, and a milk bottle. Photographing, processing, enlarging, examining ...

Burns and Ryder sat in their office, dog-tired, waiting. Knowing in their hearts that it was a pointless wait. Sometimes one got a break—but this was clutching at straws ...

Ryder got up and began to pace. To and fro, to and fro ...

Burns said, 'Cheer up, Sergeant. I'm sure it'll be a bouncing boy.'

At one o'clock there was a knock at the door and the experts came in. One of them put two photographs in front of Burns.

'Identical,' he said.

Chapter Two

Ryder said, 'But *could* he have done it, sir?'

Burns sipped the hot black coffee the sergeant had just brought down from the station canteen. 'That's the first point, isn't it . . .? On reflection, I think he could.'

'You mean the story he told you about his movements on Saturday was phoney?'

'Not unless his girl-friend and the restaurant proprietor and the waiter were all in some collective plot—which seems very unlikely.'

'So up to 1.30 a.m. he was in London?'

'I would say so.'

'Then I don't see, sir . . .'

'It doesn't necessarily make his alibi good, Sergeant. It seemed to, I know, at the start of the case—because we were misled into believing that someone removed Quarry forcibly from the hotel before murdering him at 2.30. Which Saxon certainly couldn't have done if he was in London at 1.30 . . . But now we've decided that Quarry left voluntarily, that aspect's irrelevant. We can forget the hotel and simply concentrate on the murder.'

'Yes—of course.'

'Now it's true that Saxon couldn't have killed Quarry at 2.30 a.m. *at Lowark*, because he couldn't have got there in time. But then there's never been any evidence that Quarry was killed at Lowark. Saxon might still have killed him *somewhere* at 2.30 a.m . . . In short, I'd say that his account of his movements doesn't give him an alibi any more.'

'Well, that's something.'

'So now we come to the next question. How far is the presence of Saxon's ball in the car an indication that he did the murder?'

'Are you thinking that it might have got into the car in some legitimate way, sir?'

'We've got to consider the possibility. Now let's see . . . Saxon told me when I first saw him that he'd never been driven by Quarry. He said they didn't have a social relationship, and that the only place they'd met—apart from the one visit of Saxon's to Harpenden—was in Quarry's office. That doesn't sound as though there'd have been much chance of the ball getting into the car legitimately *before* the visit.'

'And soon afterwards,' Ryder said, 'the big row broke out, and they didn't meet any more.'

Burns nodded. 'So it's that one visit we're concerned with . . . Suppose Saxon had the ball with him when he went to Harpenden, and accidentally jerked it out of his pocket at some point . . .'

'It wouldn't have been an easy thing to jerk out of a pocket, sir. Round, smooth, solid . . .'

'When he was pulling out a handkerchief, say? To mop his forehead after a sticky interview? In the drive, before he got into his car?'

'Well—perhaps . . .'

'Then someone might have picked it up later and popped it into Quarry's car—if the car had been parked near by.'

'The only print on the ball was Saxon's, sir.'

'Yes—that would take a bit of explaining.' Burns pondered. 'On balance, then, it would seem more likely that the ball got into the car on the night of the murder.'

'Much more likely.'

'If it did, there'd be little doubt that Saxon killed Quarry. Which brings us to the next question. What would his motive have been?'

'Well, sir, we know he was on bad terms with Quarry.'

'M'm . . . I wouldn't put it quite like that. We know Quarry suddenly got angry with *him*. Saxon seemed pretty indifferent about the row.'

'He could have been hiding his feelings. If he'd killed Quarry, that's just what he would have done.'

'Very true . . .'

'And where there's anger on one side, sir, there's always the chance of more under the surface than one can see. Especially when the anger seems extreme.'

'What are you thinking of, Sergeant?'

'I was just wondering whether Quarry had something more than a loss on shares to be angry about.'

'Like what?'

'Like something Saxon had found out about him . . . Suppose, for instance, Quarry had been up to something shady, something criminal. To do with his share portfolio, maybe. Suppose Saxon asked him some question, or dropped some remark, which led Quarry to believe he might find out the truth. A thing like that could account for the outburst over Saxon's bad advice—which would have been an excuse—and for Quarry breaking off relations with the firm and asking for his papers to be returned. He could have been shutting down on Saxon—preventing the possibility of any further discoveries.'

Burns nodded. 'Good—so far. But it doesn't explain how the two men got on killing terms.'

'It might, sir. Suppose this break with the firm came too late. Suppose Saxon had *already* discovered enough to expose Quarry.'

'Ah—blackmail again, eh?'

'It made a certain amount of sense, sir, even when we were only discussing it as a notion in the air. Now we've got an actual person in mind—who could actually have had an opportunity to find something out. What's more, I can see Saxon as a blackmailer—he struck me as a pretty tough cookie under that smooth manner of his.'

'Yes—I rather agree with that. All right—on with your theory! What happened next?'

'Well, Saxon got to work on Quarry, demanding money. Quarry realized that his freedom and career were at stakes—and maybe his marriage, too. So he said he'd pay up, and he made a secret appointment to meet Saxon on Saturday night. But he didn't intend to pay—he intended to kill. So, just to be on the safe side, he fixed up his complicated alibi for the weekend. They met as arranged, and things went wrong for Quarry, and it was he who got killed—without Saxon meaning to kill him. Just the way we discussed it before.'

'And then Saxon drove the body to Lowark?'

'That's right, to suggest a factory motive. He'd have known all about the strike from the papers. Everybody did.'

'And somehow he got back to his own car. Wherever it had been left.'

'Somehow, yes.'

'M'm . . . The trouble here, of course, is that while the people we talked about earlier as possible suspects—Driscoll, and your first hypothetical blackmailer—were local men, Saxon isn't. He'd have known about the strike, but he'd hardly have known about 'Wanderer', and the track, and the hikers. Wouldn't he just have dumped the car near Lowark and cleared off?'

Ryder thought for a moment—and slowly nodded. 'I guess he would, sir . . . Well—it was a try.'

'It wasn't a bad try,' Burns said. 'We're both groping—and the pieces of this jigsaw are only going to fit once—when we get them *all* right . . . I wouldn't rule out your blackmail angle, Sergeant. If Saxon killed Quarry—and that ball in the car certainly suggests that he might have done—there must have been a meeting somewhere, and it must have arisen out of something secret in their relationship. So it's simply a question of going on probing. It looks as though we'll have to take another trip to town.'

'I'm in court tomorrow, sir—the Beagle affair. No chance of getting out of that.'

'Oh, I'd forgotten . . . Well, I'll go on my own tomorrow and make some more inquiries . . .' Burns glanced at his watch. It was two o'clock. 'I mean to-day,' he said, with sudden weariness.

At three o'clock on the following afternoon, the superintendent was sitting in the plush offices of Keenan, Hall and Webb, Quarry's former stockbrokers, facing the senior partner, Arthur Richards.

'The question I'd like to put to you, sir,' Burns said, 'is whether some illegal action by a broker's client might become apparent to the broker as a result of their business association.'

Richards looked thoughtfully at the policeman. 'It's not easy to imagine such a situation, Superintendent . . . Of course, if a client were stupid enough to produce, say, forged share certificates, that might well become known to his broker. But in general, I would say that the answer to your question is "most improbable". Obviously there are plenty of ways in which a financier or an industrialist can break the law—it happens only too often—but an accountant or a solicitor would be more likely to learn of an irregularity than a broker.'

'I see . . . I'm a child in these matters, you understand—but I had wondered if any hint of irregularity had ever come to light in Robert Quarry's dealings with your firm. Something that your Mr Saxon might have noticed.'

'Good heavens, no,' Richards said. 'If there had been the slightest irregularity, Saxon would have mentioned it. We've always found him a most reliable and trustworthy member of the firm.'

'M'm . . . The reason I wondered, sir, was because some correspondence I saw between yourselves and Quarry suggested to me that you let him go rather easily. Quarry was presumably quite a valued client—or would have been when the market started to rise again—yet you certainly didn't press him to change his mind about leaving you. In fact, it seemed to me from the letters I read that you parted company with him rather thankfully . . . There was just this thought in my mind that perhaps you had some more potent reason for ending the association than the correspondence disclosed.'

Richards smiled. 'We certainly had nothing against him as far as any irregularities were concerned—far from it. I'm sure that Quarry was a man of the utmost financial integrity. But the fact is, he was a most unreasonable man. His complaints about Saxon were quite unjustified. Brokers don't pretend to be founts of absolute wisdom—they can only take a view about a market or a company, and they're often wrong. The expert, Superintendent, is the most fallible of all creatures. A man in Quarry's position, with years of experience, must have known that. His sudden, savage attack on Saxon was most irrational. And quite aside from that, he was a very demanding type of man—and very ungrateful . . .'

'In what way ungrateful, sir?'

'Well, there was that Saturday visit that Saxon made to his home. Quarry asked specially for the visit—in fact, he pressed us. We appreciated that he was a very busy man, but it was an unusual request and very much a concession on our part—and even more on the part of Saxon, who was required to give up his Saturday morning. And what happened? Saxon arrived at Quarry's home sharp at eleven o'clock to keep the appointment—only to find that the fellow wasn't there.'

'Really?'

'Yes, he'd gone out early in his car and it had got stuck in a lane, miles from anywhere. One couldn't blame him for that, of course, but when he finally did get home after keeping Saxon waiting for nearly two hours he was in a filthy temper, barely civil, and didn't even invite Saxon to share a bite of lunch. A couple of weeks after that, we had this very abusive letter—and we felt it was the last straw. We simply preferred not to deal with him any more.'

For several moments Burns sat absolutely still, staring at Richards. A large piece of the jigsaw had slipped unexpectedly into place—and the emerging picture was horrible.

Slowly, he got to his feet. 'Well, thank you, Mr Richards,' he said. 'I find it difficult to tell you how helpful you've been to me.'

Five minutes later he was on his way north—to Lowark, and the Driscolls' home.

Chapter Three

Burns said, 'When I last talked to you and your wife, Mr Driscoll, you both gave me the impression that you believed Robert and Alma Quarry had an excellent relationship. Is that your considered belief—or would you care to qualify it in any way?'

'It's certainly mine,' Driscoll said. 'I never knew a married couple more devoted to each other.'

'What about you, Mrs Driscoll?'

Betty hesitated. 'Well, if I'm to be absolutely honest,' she said, 'I think I'd put it a little differently. Alma always seemed to be devoted to Robert, that's true. But Robert sometimes struck me as being—well, you could almost call it *besotted* about Alma. He could scarcely bear to have her out of his sight.'

'Oh, come,' Driscoll said, 'not besotted. Deeply in love—and why not?'

'I'm not blaming him, darling. After all, he *was* much older than Alma, and she certainly is lovely. I suppose it isn't surprising that he drooled, rather. But I wouldn't care for all that heavy attentiveness myself. Too much of a strain.'

'Well, I think you're going rather far—but he certainly was nuts about her. I remember that time we went to Scarborough, he and I . . . When was it, Betty? That dinner at Alford's?'

'About the middle of September, wasn't it?'

'That's right. Alma had always gone everywhere with Robert until then—they'd been inseparable since their marriage. But that weekend she had a migraine or something, and couldn't come. Well, Robert telephoned her at Harpenden after the dinner. Quite late, it was—around 11.30, I should think—and he was terribly worried and upset because he couldn't get a reply. It turned out afterwards that the poor girl had taken a sleeping pill and hadn't heard the phone ring. Absolutely nothing to fuss about, you see. But Robert was almost beside himself at the time, I remember. Extraordinary!'

Burns nodded gravely. 'Did Mr Quarry give you any idea why Mrs Quarry didn't accompany him on this last trip?'

'Yes—he said he'd decided it was a bit hard on her, being toted around on a business and shooting weekend when she wasn't much interested in either.'

'Were you surprised?'

'Well, I was a bit, actually. He'd never taken that line before.'

'It was his initiative, was it?'

'That's what I gathered. But I'm sure it suited Alma very well, too.'

'M'm ... I understand from Mrs Quarry that she's a New Zealander by upbringing.'

'That's right,' Betty said. 'She only came here just over a year ago.'

'She doesn't appear to have any of the accent one associates with "down under".'

'Oh, she got rid of it, Superintendent, if she ever had it. She's an actress, you know. She'd have had to.'

'You mean she's a trained actress?'

'Well, she told me she went to acting school. I don't think she'd pretend she was ever marvellous—but she has appeared in public—and I believe she was on TV somewhere.'

'That's very interesting ... Do you happen to know how she came to meet Mr Quarry in the first place?'

'She was modelling for one of the company's publicity campaigns—isn't that right, John? Robert happened to look in when they were shooting, and he fell for her on the spot. He went all out to get her—and within two weeks they were married.'

'Quite a blitzkrieg, eh?'

'Oh, Robert never did things by halves.'

'Was Mrs Quarry a successful model?'

'Well, it depends what you mean by success. She was a competent one, I'm sure. She had the looks and the figure, and her bit of dramatic training would have helped. I would say that she *could* have been a success, if marriage hadn't cut her career short. But I don't suppose she regretted giving it up.'

'I don't suppose she did,' Burns said.

There was a slightly awkward silence. Then Driscoll said, 'What exactly are you driving at, Superintendent, with these questions? Or oughtn't we to ask?'

'At the moment, sir, I'm afraid I can't say anything. But I'm grateful to you for answering so frankly . . . Oh, there is one more thing.' Burns turned to Betty.

'Yes?' she said.

'At the Quarrys' home I met a woman—a "daily", she said she was. But no one else . . . Did the Quarrys have no servants living in? No *au pair*? It's a big house.'

'They had someone until a few weeks ago,' Betty said. 'A Spanish girl, but she left. They were trying to replace her, but you know how difficult it is these days.'

'So there was just the "daily"?'

'That's all.'

'Every day?'

'I don't really know. Five days a week, I believe. That's the usual thing these days. People like to have their weekends free, don't they?'

'They do indeed,' Burns said.

Ryder was waiting at headquarters, expecting a telephone call from the superintendent, not his arrival. Burns joined him in the office, looking grim. Any resemblance to an ageing cherub had vanished.

'Well—how did you get on in court, Sergeant?'

Ryder shrugged. 'We got the verdict, sir. Beagle was given twelve months—suspended sentence.'

'H'm. In the old days they used to suspend *people*. Now they suspend sentences. I'm not sure it's an improvement.'

Ryder looked searchingly at his chief. How did *you* get on, sir?'

'I talked to the brokers. Nothing on the financial front . . . I've just been seeing the Driscolls again.'

'I wondered why you were back so soon. Has something new turned up?'

'It certainly has, Sergeant. I learned today that Alma Quarry lied to me.'

'Lied to you? What about?'

'About herself and Saxon. When I talked to her a few days ago about the Saxon correspondence I found in the house, I asked her what Saxon was like. She said—and I'm quoting her exact words "I only saw him for a moment or two." It now appears that her husband was out somewhere, having car trouble, and didn't get back till lunchtime. It was a Saturday, so there were no domestics around. Which almost certainly means that Alma spent two hours in the house alone with Saxon.'

'Good lord!'

'It's inconceivable, of course, that she didn't talk to him. A good-looking, presentable man. Nothing else to occupy either of them. And why not? What's wrong with a nice long chat? So why did she lie?'

'Sounds like a sense of guilt, sir.'

'That's how it seems to me. It was an unthinking mistake on her part, no doubt—a defensive reaction to an innocent question she'd have done better to answer frankly. Fortunately, everyone makes mistakes . . . I think, Sergeant, we've now got to consider the possibility that something pretty big started up between those two during that couple of hours—and that they've been having an affair ever since.'

There was silence for a count of five. Then Ryder said, 'Well, that changes the case more than somewhat.'

'It does, doesn't it? In the light of a possible liaison between those two, I've been giving a bit more thought to Saturday night's movements. Suddenly, they're greatly simplified . . . We start from the point that Saxon was in London at 1.30 a.m. So he couldn't have killed Quarry at 2.30 a.m. unless he encountered him at some point within an hour's journey of London. Right?'

'Right, sir.'

'Now since we've no reason to believe that Quarry would have wanted anything to do with Saxon after he quarrelled with him over the shares; and if, as seems possible, Saxon had meanwhile been secretly liaising with Quarry's wife, it would appear unlikely that any meeting that took place would have been by prior arrangement and agreement.'

'Most unlikely, sir.'

'So that brings us to the sixty-four thousand dollar question. In the light of this possible affair between Saxon and Alma, *where* would Saxon and Quarry have been most likely to encounter each other without prior arrangement, within an hour's drive of London?'

There was fractional pause. Then Ryder said, 'At the Quarrys' house?'

Burns nodded. 'A highly intelligent guess, Sergeant Now let's see how those mileage figures fit.'

Ryder looked up from the map he'd been studying.

'Well, sir, I make it 182 miles from the Moor View Hotel to the Harpenden house—364 for the double journey. If Quarry wound back the speedo that much from the 36,513 it registered at the hotel after the service, there'd have been 36,149 on the clock when he set off.'

'Yes . . .?

'And we're now supposing,' Ryder went on, 'that the car then did 182 miles from the hotel to the house, plus 108 miles from the house to Lowark—that's 290 miles altogether. So at Lowark the speedo should have registered 36,149 plus 290—equals 36,439.'

'In fact, it registered 36,459,' Burns said. 'Twenty more.'

'Which could easily be accounted for by Quarry winding back a bit *less* than his projected double journey—as a precaution to cover his local runaround or a slightly longer route than the one he'd measured. So that's all okay.'

'And if Quarry had actually completed the double journey he'd planned,' Burns said, 'the speedo would have registered something over the 36,501 recorded at the time of the service—so no one would have had any cause for suspicion because of a reduced reading, and at the same time there'd have been clear evidence that he hadn't travelled any great distance since the service. In fact, if all had gone according to plan, he'd have got clean away with his deception.'

'No doubt about it.'

'Right . . . Now let's consider the timing. How does that work out?'

'Well, I reckon 3 1/2 hours from the hotel to Harpenden would be a fair estimate.'

Burns nodded. That's roughly what it took me in the other direction.'

'So if Quarry had left the hotel, say, at 11 p.m., he could have been at the house at 2.30 a.m.—just in time to get knocked off. And if he hadn't been knocked off, he could have been back at the hotel before daybreak with time to spare.'

Burns nodded again. 'How about Saxon?'

'If Saxon killed Quarry at 2.30 a.m., he could have got the body to Lowark by 5 a.m. and been back at his flat by around 7.30 a.m.—again, before daybreak.'

'Good,' Burns said. 'Now I suggest we go over the whole case from the beginning, and try to get the complete picture . . . Let's have some coffee sent down.'

It was about an hour later that Ryder sat back in his chair and said, 'That's it, then.' They had discussed everything—the main events and the minutiae. 'All points covered, sir—no loose ends. It looks pretty good to me.'

'It looks fine,' Burns agreed. 'But now we've got to prove it—and that's going to be the toughest job yet.'

'Not enough solid evidence, sir?'

'There's almost no evidence. There's the lie—but it's Alma's word against mine, with no witnesses, so we shan't get far with that . . . And there's the ball. Everything else is theory.'

'The evidence of the ball seems pretty damning.'

'I'm not so sure, Sergeant. I'm beginning to think it could be explained away.'

'How, sir?'

'Well, there's a new factor to be taken into account since we last discussed the ball, don't forget—Alma's complicity. Suppose she said she found the ball in the drive that Saturday afternoon—after Saxon's visit. When she was weeding the garden— *in gloves*. Suppose she said she dropped it through the window of the Rover, which happened to be standing close by in the drive at the time—and then forgot about it . . . The presence of the ball in the car would be innocently explained. So would the lack of any prints but Saxon's . . . Where would we be then?'

Ryder pulled a face. 'Up the creek, I guess.'

'Exactly. It would be the end of the case.'

'So what do we do, sir?'

Burns took out his space pipe, and began to unscrew the bowl. 'Well,' he said, 'I think our only hope is a well-planned confrontation—and in the next hour or two we'll work out our tactics in detail . . . Broadly speaking, I'd say the plan will be to foresee and forestall the obvious lines of defence. To try and close the escape routes before anyone realizes they're going to be needed. Leaving, perhaps, just one open, with some nasty traps at the end of it . . .'

Ryder grinned. 'It should be an interesting session.'

'Yes—whichever way it goes . . . Fortunately, we start with a couple of things in our favour. Saxon can't have any notion the ball was in the car—in fact he can't have missed it—or he'd never have volunteered the information that put us on to his handy private doctor. Which means we'll be a vital jump ahead. Not knowing about the ball, he'll be anxious to go on disclaiming any knowledge of the Rover—so we may be able to get some useful admissions that he won't be able to go back on.'

Ryder nodded. 'I get it.'

'And the second thing we'll have in our favour,' Burns said, 'is the unnerving effect of guilt—assuming, of course, that our theory is right and that those two *are* guilty. If they did plan Quarry's death, they'll be under an enormous strain at the showdown—having to act a part all the time, having to pretend they're virtual strangers to each other, not knowing from moment to moment what's going to be flung at them. The shocks they'll get are bound to upset them. In that sort of atmosphere, there's always the chance that one of them will crack . . .'

Alice answered the phone. 'Four-two-nine-eight-seven . . . Oh, it's you, dear. Where are you?'

'I'm in Lowark,' Burns said. 'I drove up this afternoon. Now I'm off back to London. I'll be at the same pub as before.'

'Oh . . . You're sure you're not overdoing it, Joe?'

'No, I'm fine.'

'How are things going?'

'Well—we've got our eyes on a couple of promising fish.'

'Have you really?'

'Yes. We'll be making a few casts tomorrow night.'

'Oh, good. Well. I wish you luck. You know you've only got two more days, don't you?'

'It'll be enough,' Burns said. 'Either we'll land our fish tomorrow or they'll be off the hook for good. Whichever way it goes, the case will be over. For me, at any rate. You can start to pack.'

PART FIVE

Chapter One

The showdown began, quietly and almost imperceptibly, at seven o'clock on the following evening. As Burns and Constable Williams, parked outside The Hillocks, saw the distant double flash of Ryder's headlights signalling his approach, they turned into the drive to keep the appointment with Alma Quarry that Burns had arranged by telephone earlier in the day. The time seemed to have come, he'd said, when he should inform her about the progress of the investigation. The invitation to her home had resulted.

Alma's reception of them—dignified, subdued, but friendly—was exactly appropriate to the occasion. A bereaved wife was to be told something about the events that had widowed her. The facts would no doubt be painful—but it was her right and her duty to hear them . . .

The policemen lingered for a moment in the hall, as Burns presented Constable Williams and courtesies were exchanged. Burns said, 'I'm glad you were able to see us, Mrs Quarry. As I hinted on the phone, we've made some progress with the case, and I felt sure you'd wish to know how far we've got . . .'

There was the sound of a car coming up the drive. Alma glanced towards the door. Burns said, 'That should be my colleague, Sergeant Ryder. I took the liberty of asking him to bring someone else along, Mrs Quarry—a man who is also interested in the case. I hope you don't mind.'

Alma looked at him in surprise. 'Well . . .' she began uncertainly.

Steps sounded outside. The bell tinkled. Alma said, 'Excuse me,' and went to the door and opened it. Sergeant Ryder and Peter Saxon were standing there in the light of the porch lamp.

Burns watched the tableau.

It was Saxon who spoke first. 'Good evening, Mrs Quarry.'

There was the slightest pause, as Alma gazed hard at him. 'Oh, hullo,' she said. 'I didn't recognize you at first . . . You came to see my husband, didn't you—about his investments?'

'That's right.'

'Please come in . . . I'm afraid I've forgotten your name.'

'Saxon. Peter Saxon.'

'Yes, of course.' Alma stood back, and the two men entered. Burns introduced Sergeant Ryder, and they all moved into the sitting-room. Ryder was carrying a small attaché case. Burns had his bag.

Saxon said, in a puzzled tone, 'Your sergeant, Superintendent, tells me you want to give me some information about Mr Quarry's death. I'm far from clear how it can have anything to do with me, or why it should have been necessary for me to come here.' He looked across at Alma. 'As far as I'm concerned, Mrs Quarry, it's an intrusion—and I apologize.'

'That's quite all right,' Alma said. 'I expect the superintendent has his reasons.' She was pale—but there was clearly nothing wrong with her nerve so far. 'Shall we all sit down?'

Burns said, 'Before I go into details about the discoveries we've made, there are one or two points about Mr Quarry's earlier movements that I'd like to clear up . . . Mr Saxon, would you take your mind back to that Saturday morning when you called on Mr Quarry here? I believe you arrived at about eleven o'clock—is that right?'

'Quite right, Superintendent.'

'And Mrs Quarry let you in?'

'Yes.'

'Mr Quarry wasn't at home?'

'No—he'd been held up somewhere.'

'What time did he return?'

'Just before one—wasn't it, Mrs Quarry?'

Alma nodded.

'A long wait, Mr Saxon. You must have wondered what had happened.'

'Naturally.'

'And you could give him no explanation, Mrs Quarry?'

'All I knew,' Alma said, 'was that my husband had driven up to the common for his usual Saturday morning walk.'

'Were you worried?'

'Not really—Robert was a very careful driver. I thought perhaps he'd had a puncture.'

'So you continued to wait, Mr Saxon.'

'Of course. Mr Quarry might have returned at any moment—obviously I had to wait and see.'

'No doubt you were offered some hospitality?'

'Mrs Quarry was kind enough to produce some sherry.'

'And she had a glass with you, I assume?'

'I'd hardly have left Mr Saxon to drink alone,' Alma said.

'Quite so, Mrs Quarry . . . What puzzles me is why you told me the other day that you saw Mr Saxon for only a moment or two on that Saturday morning.'

Alma stared at him. 'I told you nothing of the sort, Superintendent . . . You asked me what Mr Saxon was like, and I described him, and said I didn't know much about him and if you wanted more information you'd better ask at his office. That's all.'

'My recollection is different,' Burns said.

'Then you must have misheard or misunderstood. How could I possibly have said I only saw Mr Saxon for a moment or two when he was here for two hours?'

A glance passed between Burns and Ryder.

'Well, a mistake was obviously made by someone,' Burns said mildly. 'We'll leave it at that . . . Let's get back now to Mr Quarry—and his eventual return home. Just before one, you told me, Mr Saxon?'

'Yes.'

'Two hours late.'

'Yes.'

'What explanation did he give you?'

'He said he'd had trouble with his car. That's all.'

'He was rather curt, was he?'

'He was a little curt, yes,' Saxon said, with an apologetic glance at Alma.

'Did the car show any sign of trouble?'

'I wouldn't know, Superintendent. I didn't see his car.'

'You mean it wasn't around?'

'I mean I wouldn't have known if it had been. I know nothing about his car—I never saw it. There was no car visible when I was here. I suppose he put it in his garage when he got back . . .'

Burns gave an inward sigh of satisfaction. One escape hatch was firmly blocked.

'Look, Superintendent,' Saxon went on, 'what *is* all this about?. You bring me here, at great inconvenience to myself—and some embarrassment, I'm sure, to Mrs Quarry—and you ask all these trivial questions that seem to have no bearing on anything. I understood from the sergeant that it was you who were going to supply the information. If not, what am I doing here?'

'You're helping the police with their inquiries,' Burns said. 'If you don't wish to, you don't have to—it's entirely up to you. But I'd have thought that as a good citizen you'd have had no objection . . . And the same, of course, applies to Mrs Quarry.'

Saxon shrugged. 'Well, it all seems a complete waste of time to me—but I suppose you know what you're doing.'

'I do, indeed,' Burns said. He could see a trace of moisture on Saxon's forehead that hadn't been there a moment ago. Alma, on the settee, was sitting as still as a statue. That euphemistic phrase about helping the police with their inquiries had evidently done its work. The pair had been stonewalling until this point. Now they were fully alerted—and tensely waiting.

Unhurriedly, Burns resumed. 'If I may, then, I'll continue with my questions . . . I'd like you to think back, Mr Saxon, to the injury you sustained to your finger. In July, I believe you said it happened.'

'That's right.'

'Can you recall the exact date?'

'No—but it was early in the month. In the first few days.'

'How long did the cracked bone take to heal?'

'About a couple of weeks.'

'So it was knitted by, say, the third week in July.'

'About then.'

'What was the treatment, Mr Saxon?'

'Immobilization, first of all. Then physiotherapy exercises.'

'What form did the exercises take?'

'I had to squeeze a small rubber ball.'

'I see . . . And how long did you continue these exercises?'

'Oh—for a week or ten days.'

'Not longer?'

'No . . . it was all a bit of a bore.'

'By the beginning of August, then, the finger was giving you no more trouble?'

'Only when someone shook hands with me rather hard!'

'Quite so . . . I had wondered if you occupied any of your two hours here by exercising with the ball. But from what you say, it would appear not.'

'No, I'd discarded it by then.'

Burns turned to Alma. 'Then naturally you wouldn't have known about this rubber ball, Mrs Quarry?'

'No,' she said.

'You certainly never saw it at any time?'

'How could I?'

'Exactly—how could you . . .?' Burns' expression was almost benevolent as the second door clanged tight.

'Where is the ball now, Mr Saxon?'

Saxon shrugged. 'I've no idea. Does it matter? I'm still completely baffled by these questions.'

Burns opened his bag and took out a small plastic box with a sealed polythene top. Inside the box, a small rubber ball rested on a base of cotton wool like a corpse on a catafalque. Burns passed the box to Saxon. 'Is that the ball?'

Saxon gave it a casual glance—and shrugged again.

'How would I know? It looks similar—that's all I can tell you.'

Burns took the box back. 'I suppose there's no point in showing it to you, Mrs Quarry, is there—as you never saw it?'

'No,' said Alma, white and tense.

'M'm ... Well, I'm not surprised you should think this ball similar to your own, Mr Saxon. Actually, it has your fingerprints on it.'

'Oh?' Saxon was visibly sweating again, 'How do you know they're mine? No one ever took my fingerprints.'

'You were putting out a milk bottle, Mr Saxon, when we came to see you. I borrowed it.'

'I see . . . All right—so they're my prints, and it's my ball. I didn't deny it, you know—I just wasn't sure ... Where did you find it—and why is it so important?'

'It was found,' Burns said, 'on the floor of Robert Quarry's car after he was murdered. That's why it's important.'

There was a moment of silence—broken dramatically by Alma. 'Oh, *Peter*,' she murmured—and slumped across the settee in a faint.

She was out for less than a minute. As she stirred, Constable Williams fetched a glass of water from the kitchen and held it to her lips. A faint trace of colour returned to her cheeks. Saxon sat motionless, ignoring her, ignoring everything except his danger and his problem.

'Well, Mr Saxon,' Burns said, 'how do you explain the ball?'

Saxon shook his head. 'At the moment, Superintendent, I can't explain it.'

'You mean, perhaps, that you can't explain it in any way satisfactory to yourself—and that I can understand. After all, you did say this evening in the presence of three police witnesses that you'd never even seen Quarry's car—let alone been in it. And you said you didn't have the ball on the only occasion you came here. And Mrs Quarry said she'd never seen it ... So there *are* a few difficulties, aren't there? And you, Mrs Quarry—how do you explain that sudden fainting attack? And being on first-name terms with a man you saw only once before in your life, for two hours? A man whose surname, even, you appeared tonight not to be able to remember.'

Alma looked helplessly at Saxon.

'All right,' Burns said, 'I've no wish to go on playing cat-and-mouse with you. What was little more than an unsubstantiated theory when I came here this evening would now seem to be supported by a certain amount of evidence. Let me tell you, on the basis of the information I have, just how that theory goes . . .' Burns paused for a moment, framing in his mind the words which by the end would seem to offer a partial and tempting way out. 'It goes something like this . . . Mrs Quarry was disappointed in her marriage to an older man. She discovered her husband to be possessive and domineering. She became lonely and unhappy. When she'd been married for nearly a year, Mr Saxon chanced to call at the house. By chance, he spent two hours alone with her. Mr Saxon was a good-looking, lively and amusing man of her own generation. Mrs Quarry was ripe for an affair. When they parted, it was with the understanding that they would meet again. Which they did. Soon they had fallen deeply in love. They desperately wanted to be together. But the opportunities were few, and they both felt frustrated and wretched. Then, last weekend, Robert Quarry went north alone. He indicated in various ways that he intended to stay up there for the whole weekend. So Mr Saxon arranged to spend Saturday night here with Mrs Quarry. During the night, Quarry returned unexpectedly. In the encounter that followed, Mr Saxon killed him. On the face of it, that was murder. Afterwards Mr Saxon drove Quarry's body to Lowark, in an attempt to cover up the killing. It may well be that the attendant at some petrol station on the route may remember seeing Quarry's car. And it was during that drive that Mr Saxon's ball got into the car . . . Anyway, that's the theory . . .'

There were no protests, no outbursts. Not a sound from anyone disturbed the silence in the room. Alma and Saxon sat as though hypnotized. Burns moved smoothly to the completion of his ploy.

'All this, of course, you may know. That depends on whether the theory is true or not. But now I'm going to tell you something that I'm sure you *don't* know. All those arrangements that Quarry made when he was in Yorkshire—all the information he put out indicating that he proposed to stay there till Sunday—had a dual purpose. One was to convince you that he wouldn't be coming back—so that you'd feel safe to spend the night together if you wished. The other was to give himself an alibi—which he went to great lengths to achieve. Not only did he spread it around that he intended to stay up there—and allow himself to be seen in bed by a waiter as late as 10.45 on Saturday night, to provide corroborative detail—he also wound back the speedometer of his car to conceal the journey he was going to make, to prove that he had stayed up north. And why did he need this alibi? Because he was an extravagantly jealous and possessive man, a man of extreme and violent temperament; because he expected to find you together; and because then he intended to kill you both.'

Burns paused again. 'It is now my duty to tell you that, on the evidence available, I suspect you both of being concerned in the murder of Robert Quarry. I must therefore caution you. You are not obliged to say anything unless you wish to do so, but what you say may be put into writing and given in evidence . . . Before you decide whether to speak or not, I should like to say just this. I can offer you no inducements—but in the light of the information I have just given you about Quarry there would appear to be some possibility of extenuating circumstances. Obviously a full account of what happened, freely volunteered at this stage, would carry more weight in a court than anything you felt obliged to say later . . . Now it's entirely up to you.'

Saxon looked at Alma. Alma looked at Saxon.

'I think, darling,' Saxon said, 'we'd better tell the superintendent just what happened . . .'

Ryder took a battery tape-recorder from his attaché case and set it up. Constable Williams sat down at a table and opened his notebook. Ryder switched on the recorder.

Burns said, to get it on tape: 'I am cautioning you again, Mr

Saxon, that you are not obliged to say anything, and that anything you do say will be taken down and may be used in evidence.'

Saxon nodded. 'I understand.'

'Then go ahead.'

Saxon leaned forward and addressed Burns in a low, earnest voice, as though he could barely contain his inner sincerity. 'I did kill Robert Quarry,' he said. 'But it wasn't murder—it was self-defence.'

Burns inclined his head in a way he hoped was encouraging.

'Much of what you said is true, Superintendent. Alma and I fell desperately in love after my visit to see Quarry. The fact is, she'd made a terrible mistake in her marriage. Her husband turned out quite differently from what she'd expected. It wasn't just that he was possessive and jealous—he was harsh and overbearing and often cruel in manner. Not to her, but to other people—his colleagues, his workpeople—and she couldn't stand it. I was terribly concerned for her, and we met and talked about everything, and—well, we just fell in love, as people do. And of course it *was* frustrating—we had to meet secretly, under great difficulties, just for an hour or two . . . Then, last weekend, it did look as though we could be on our own, and feel safe. Everything pointed to the fact that Quarry would be staying in Yorkshire till Sunday. So on Saturday night I came here, and Alma and I went to bed . . .'

Saxon reached for the water that Williams had brought, and took a sip. Then he resumed:

'Well, some time after two o'clock in the morning we heard a noise downstairs. It didn't occur to us that it could be Quarry—we thought it was a burglar, or perhaps someone from the factory who'd got it in for Quarry and had come to do him harm. I slipped on a shirt and trousers and went out on the landing. I could hear movements in the sitting-room downstairs. The door was ajar and there was a light showing. I looked around for something I could defend myself with. All I could see was a draught-excluder at the foot of the attic door. It was a sort of long sandbag, quite heavy. I doubled it up, and it made quite a good weapon. I crept downstairs, with Alma just behind me. I pushed the sitting-room door open, and there was a man there. He was looking at some glasses Alma and I had been drinking out of. It was Quarry—and he had a shotgun under his arm. He swung round and pointed the gun at me and started shouting. He was beside himself—yelling abuse and calling Alma everything under the sun. He said he was going to kill us both, and he moved towards us, still pointing the gun. I rushed at him, and somehow I managed to grab the gun and push it up before he could fire, and I hit him with the sandbag. He dropped to the floor, but he wasn't unconscious, and I hit him again, and we struggled—it seemed for ages. Then—well, then I found he was dead . . . And that, I swear, is how it happened. He *would* have killed us—and it *was* self-defence. I had no choice.'

'I see,' Burns said. 'And you confirm this, Mrs Quarry?'

Alma, who appeared to be crying quietly into a handkerchief, said 'Yes' in a stifled voice.

'What happened to the sandbag afterwards?'

'I think Alma put it back against the attic door,' Saxon said.

Alma raised her head, and nodded.

Burns motioned to Williams. 'Find it and bring it down, will you, Constable?'

Williams departed. In a few moments he returned with the draught-excluder. It was a slim, three-foot-long cylinder of sand, covered in dark green nylon. Burns doubled it up, grasped the two ends in one fist, and swung it through the air like a truncheon.

'Yes,' he said grimly, 'that would have been a very effective weapon. How fortunate that you thought of it, Mr Saxon . . .! So now you had Quarry's body on your hands.'

'Yes . . .'

'And you decided to dispose of it.'

'It seemed the only thing to do . . . We didn't think anyone would believe I'd killed him in self-defence. We felt we wouldn't get any sympathy or even a fair hearing—in view of the situation.'

'I can understand your anxiety . . . So what precisely did you do with the body?'

'We carried it down the drive—the two of us. I fetched the Rover from the lane, where Quarry had left it—and together we managed to get him into the boot.'

'Why did you take him to Lowark?'

'It seemed the obvious place, in view of all the trouble there'd been there. It was the sort of place where Quarry might well have got himself killed.'

'That's why you wrote "Bastard" on the car?'

'Yes . . . We were simply trying to protect ourselves.'

'Why did you go in for all those trimmings at Lowark? The arm left sticking out, the smashed clock . . .?'

'That was all to do with trying to fix an alibi.'

'What made you think you might be in need of an alibi?'

'Well, we were afraid someone might have discovered that we'd been seeing each other. There was one occasion—just one—when Alma stayed at my flat—and someone passed her on the stairs as she left in the morning. We were scared someone might remember her, and link us with Quarry's death.'

'How did you see these alibi arrangements working out? How exactly did you think they would help?'

'The way we saw it, the arrangements Quarry had made to take *us* in, by indicating his intention to stay at the hotel, would have taken *others* in, too. We didn't know then about his changing the speedometer reading, of course, or about his having actually gone to bed—but we did realize he'd done enough to show his intention to stay. And if the evidence showed he'd intended to stay, we thought the conclusion would be that he'd been taken forcibly from the hotel. Which I couldn't have done, because I could prove I'd been in London.'

'At the theatre, and at a restaurant.'

'Exactly. It seemed as though he'd positively *presented* me with an alibi—so I used it.'

'And your effort to pinpoint the time of death at 2.30 a.m.—what was the purpose of that?'

'It was just to confuse things, really. I thought the police might think he'd been killed at Lowark at 2.30—in which case I couldn't have done it.'

'How did you come to choose that particular track?'

'Well, we needed some quiet spot near Lowark where we could leave the body without any risk of being seen, but where it was likely to be discovered quite soon— and we discussed it—and Alma remembered a map she'd seen in the local paper . . .'

'The copy of the *Lowark Advertiser* that John Driscoll had sent to your husband, Mrs Quarry?'

'Yes,' Alma said.

'And she remembered about the hikers,' Saxon went on, 'and how they'd be there in the morning—and it seemed just the place . . . I do realize, Superintendent, that it all sounds horribly cold-blooded now, but we were terribly frightened about what might happen—we were really quite desperate . . .'

Burns nodded. 'I assume you drove the Rover, Mr Saxon. How did you get back?'

'Alma followed me in her own car. She waited for me by the bridge . . .'

'Behind that pile of road metal?'

'That's right. I walked back there, and she drove me home.'

'To this house?'

'Yes . . . Then I picked up my own car and drove to my flat.'

'What time did you get there?'

'About half-past seven.'

'M'm . . . Quite a night out, Mr Saxon!'

'It was appalling, Superintendent. It was terrible.'

'Yes . . . Well, now I'd like to go back a little and cover some of the points we've passed over . . . How did you and Mrs Quarry communicate after your first meeting here at the house?'

'Alma used to ring me at the office,' Saxon said, 'giving different names. Then we used to meet in our two cars—mostly up on Dunstable Downs, which was handy for her. Sometimes I'd pretend I had a client to see, and I'd take a three-hour lunch break. Sometimes Alma managed to slip away for an hour in the evening, when Quarry had some engagement. It was all most involved and unsatisfactory.'

'You would, of course, have solved your problem if Mrs Quarry had simply left her husband.'

'She did suggest that, Superintendent, but I wouldn't let her do it. There was nothing I'd have liked better—but I knew she was afraid of what he might do. I thought it would have worried her too much.'

'She would also, of course, have sacrificed a good deal of money if she'd left him. I understand she was present when Quarry drew up a will leaving the bulk of his considerable fortune to her.' Burns waited for a comment, an amendment, from Alma—but none came. Another piece of the puzzle had fallen neatly into place.

Saxon said, with a show of indignation, 'That didn't enter into it at all.'

'I see . . . Well, now, there are still a few things I'm not clear about. Quarry would hardly have gone to so much trouble to fix up an alibi for himself unless he'd been *very* suspicious of what his wife might be up to. Almost certain, in fact. Certain enough to make all preparations for a killing . . . What do you suppose made him so suspicious?'

'I think first of all,' Saxon said, 'It was finding me alone with Alma when he got back that Saturday. I think that's when the seed was sown. Maybe there was something in her manner that gave us away—I don't know . . . Then there was one very unfortunate incident early in September, when Quarry found a cigarette butt in the ashtray of Alma's car—an untipped butt, when she only smoked tipped. I don't know how we came to be so careless. Alma gave him some explanation, of course—she said she'd given a lift to someone—but I doubt if he believed it . . . . And then there was that one night I told you about when Alma stayed with me at the flat. Quarry was in Scarborough, and he rang her at home and got no answer, and she had to say next day that she'd taken a sleeping pill . . . I suppose he put all those things together and drew his conclusion.'

'Did you sense that he was suspicious, Mrs Quarry?'

'I thought he might be,' Alma said. 'His manner changed a little after those two incidents—he seemed to be watching me more than ever.'

'I thought he was suspicious,' Saxon said, 'when he suddenly got nasty about me without good reason. It seemed as though he'd cottoned on to something. I couldn't believe it was just a professional matter—it didn't make sense.'

Burns nodded. 'Tell me, why did you choose last Saturday for your assignation? Why not Friday?'

'Because on Friday we were still not sure where Quarry was. At that time he hadn't decided what hotel he was going to stay at, so we had no means of checking up on him.'

'And he'd have known that too, of course—that without a line on him you wouldn't dare risk Friday. Hence his confident plans for Saturday.'

'I suppose that's how he worked it out.'

'Why did you decide to come here, Mr Saxon, rather than have Mrs Quarry visit you? Wouldn't that have been safer?'

'Not really—at least, we didn't think so. We thought there was a chance that Quarry might ring up again during the night. We couldn't risk Alma not being there a second time.'

'Which again he might have realized?'

'Yes.'

Burns turned a page of his notes—and now his tone became sharper. 'I'd like to revert to the ball for a moment . . . You told me you stopped using the ball before your first visit to this house—yet somehow it got into the Rover when you were driving Quarry's body to Lowark. How do you suppose that happened?'

'I've been thinking about it,' Saxon said. 'I guess it must have been in a pocket of the jacket I was wearing. I remember I was very hot—after the struggle and everything—and I threw the jacket on to the back seat while I was driving. I suppose the ball must have rolled out.'

'You mean the ball was in the pocket of a suit you were constantly wearing and you hadn't noticed it—you hadn't bothered to take it out?'

'I was wearing an old sports jacket and trousers that night. The ball must have been in the pocket for a long time. It wasn't a jacket I wore very often—that's why I hadn't taken the ball out. Of course, I'm only guessing—I don't really *know* what happened.'

'Surely,' Burns said, 'you didn't go to the theatre and to a good restaurant in an old sports jacket?'

'No—I changed.'

'When did you change?'

'After I left the restaurant. I called in at my flat on the way here.'

'Just to change into old clothes, for a few hours in bed with a girl-friend—and at half-past one in the morning?'

'Well, I had to pack a few things for the night.'

'What things?'

'Toothbrush, razor and so on ... I was planning to go straight to the office in the morning.'

'In your old sports jacket?'

'I'd have dropped off at the flat to change clothes—but that's all ... Anyway, I wanted to phone Alma before I joined her, to make sure the coast was clear. The flat seemed the best place to do it.'

'M'm ... I'm bound to say, Mr Saxon, I'm a little puzzled by your actions. You'd planned to spend a night with your mistress in a comfortable bed—a very rare treat for you. You weren't expecting Quarry to come back. Yet you tell me you didn't reach the house until 2 a.m. Instead, you took another girl out to a theatre, had a leisurely meal alone in an expensive restaurant, and then wasted perhaps a further quarter of an hour in going to your flat, changing your clothes and packing some things. This all suggests to me a remarkable lack of ardour.'

'It wasn't that, Superintendent. Alma and I had both agreed it would be better to wait until two o'clock so that the neighbours would all have gone to bed and everything in the lane would be quiet. It was just a precaution.'

'I see ... By the way, when did you make that theatre arrangement?'

'On Saturday afternoon.'

'As late as that?'

‘Yes.’

‘As a result of which, and of your subsequent leisurely meal, you happened by pure chance to be able to come up with a sort of alibi.’

‘By pure chance, yes.’

‘Didn’t you have any objection to the arrangement, Mrs Quarry?’

‘No,’ Alma said. ‘I knew Peter was only filling in time until he could come to me. He had to do something.’

‘I see. I’m obviously old-fashioned . . . Well, let’s get back to the incidents at the house, shall we? It appears, Mr Saxon, that you tackled an extremely angry man who was pointing a gun at you and threatening to kill you. All you had by way of a weapon was a sandbag. That was a very brave thing to do.’

‘I didn’t think about it,’ Saxon said. ‘I could see he was going to shoot. I seemed to have no choice.’

‘Perhaps you would give me a demonstration of exactly what happened? I’ll be Quarry.’ Burns got up. ‘Now—where was I standing?’

‘A little nearer to the table,’ Saxon said. Burns moved a step or two. ‘Yes—that’s about it’

‘And I had a shotgun.’

‘Yes.’

‘Constable Williams, would you kindly get me an umbrella from the hall? I think I saw one there . . .’

Williams went out, and returned after a moment with a man’s umbrella. Burns took it from him.

‘Was the shotgun “broken”, Mr Saxon—or was it held ready for firing?’

‘Ready for firing,’ Saxon said.

‘Like this?’ Burns held the umbrella in the crook of his right arm, the ferrule pointing at Saxon.

‘About like that.’

‘Good . . . Now you and Mrs Quarry have just appeared at the door. I point the gun at you and say I’m going to kill you. You rush forward and knock up the gun. Show me, please, just how you did it.’

Saxon hurled himself across the room, seized the umbrella with his right hand, and forced the ferrule upwards.

'But surely,' Burns said, 'you'd have had the sandbag in your right hand?'

'Oh, yes—of course . . . I must have used my left hand to knock up the gun. Everything happened so quickly, it's difficult to remember.'

'I'm sure it is . . . So then, if I understood you, you hit Quarry with the sandbag, and he fell. And the two of you struggled together on the floor?'

'Yes.'

'Quarry was an extremely powerful man, Mr Saxon, You appear to me to be rather a—slim man. Not impressively muscular, shall we say. Yet in this struggle you received no injuries?'

'I suppose I was lucky,' Saxon said. 'And, looking back, I think my first blow with the sandbag must have weakened him more than I realized.'

'The medical report on Quarry shows that he was struck on the head several times. In fact, that he was savagely battered. He was then asphyxiated by heavy pressure on his windpipe. Perhaps by a knee or a foot . . . What have you to say about that?'

'I don't remember, Superintendent—I honestly don't remember. If you've ever faced a loaded gun yourself, you must know what it feels like. I was afraid of Quarry—I was in a panic. I knew he was far stronger than I was. I knew it was him or me. I suppose I went a bit berserk. Whatever I did, I didn't mean to kill him. I simply wanted to prevent him killing me.'

Burns turned to Alma. 'Presumably you were watching all this time, Mrs Quarry. What did you do?'

'I couldn't do anything, Superintendent. I was terrified.'

'Your husband was being killed before your eyes. You didn't attempt to intervene? Not even when he was clearly unconscious—when the struggle was over?'

'I tell you, I was so frightened I couldn't move. It was so awful.'

'M'm . . . Well, I've only a few more questions now. Going back a little, Mr Saxon, you say that you heard an intruder downstairs—and it turned out to be Quarry. How do you suppose he got into the house?'

'He had his key, of course.'

'So he just walked in through the front door?'

'Yes.'

'You mean to tell me you were sleeping with another man's wife in that man's house, and you didn't take the precaution of using the double lock that I noticed on the door? The very elementary precaution . . .?'

'I didn't think of it . . .'

'Remarkable . . .! And now for a final word about your Lowark trip. You had just, as you say, inadvertently killed a man and you were in a complete panic. To get to Lowark, and back before daylight, you must have left here almost immediately after the killing. You and Mrs Quarry travelled in separate cars, so you had no opportunity for discussion on the way . . . In a matter of a few minutes, therefore, you were able to decide on Lowark as the disposal place; to learn from Mrs Quarry all about the local paper and the sketch map and "Wanderer" and the hikers; to think up your plan about leaving the arm out, and turning the car round; and get the body to the drive, and the car to the drive, and the body in the boot . . . All in a few minutes. Is that what you're saying?'

'It's what happened.'

'What did you do with the gun, Mr Saxon?'

'I took it to the car, and "broke" it, and put the cartridges back in the box that I found in the boot, and the gun back in its case.'

'It's strange, then, that none of your fingerprints are on the gun—which you wrested from Quarry, and carried to the car, and emptied of its shells, and subsequently re-packed in its case . . . Or were you already wearing gloves when you crept downstairs?'

'Of course not . . . I wiped the gun.'

'The whole of it? The barrels and the stock?'

'Yes.'

'Then it's even stranger,' Burns said, 'that Quarry's prints *are* on the gun . . .' He motioned to Williams. 'Will you take Mr Saxon into another room, Constable? And keep a very close eye on him.'

Burns looked at Alma. 'I'm going to repeat my earlier caution, Mrs Quarry. You are not obliged to say anything, but anything you say will be taken down and may be used in evidence. And I'm not inviting you to say anything. I'm going to *tell* you . . .

'It's now absolutely clear to me that you and Saxon plotted together to murder your husband, whom you never cared for in the slightest. Both of you had the strongest of motives. You wanted to live together, but you also wanted to live together on Quarry's money, which you'd married him for—most of which you believed would come to you at his death. You were wrong about that, as it happens, because in fact he scrapped his earlier will—ostensibly on the ground that he didn't wish to leave any money to his niece. His real reason was that he no longer wished to leave money to you—which of course was why he didn't tell you about his action. As far as you knew, you were virtually his sole heiress . . .

'You had probably discussed the possibility of getting rid of him quite early in your acquaintance with Saxon—but you couldn't see a safe way. With a motive like yours, you were bound to come under suspicion of involvement if he were found murdered within striking distance of you. What you needed was an alibi. And, suddenly, it seemed that you'd been presented with one . . .

'I can only guess at the sequence and gradual unfolding of your plans in the day or two before the murder. First, when Quarry went away, there would probably have been no more than the hope of a long, undisturbed night with your lover. Then there came the dawning suspicion on your part that it was all too good to be true—that Quarry might intend to return unexpectedly and catch you. You knew he was crazily jealous, and that he already suspected you. You knew it was he who had initiated his trip. You knew he had made no great efforts to persuade you to go with him, though he usually did. You sensed that his letter to you from York, with its defensive explanation of why he was writing and not phoning, was intended to show that he was actually up north. It may well have struck you that to get that letter off as he did, he would have had to go to the hotel for stationery, and back to York to post it—a distance of twenty-four miles in all and a surprising effort for a man who was supposed to be resting. You sensed that his late phone call on Saturday night had the same object as the letter—to allay any doubts. You sensed that he was overdoing the talk about his shooting plans. Above all, you doubted if he'd have gone again to that hotel you'd both disliked, except for one reason—that it was an easy place to slip out of unobserved. In short, you had over the weekend a steadily strengthening belief that he did intend to return . . .

'At first, no doubt, you merely thought—dare we risk a night together if he may return? But then you thought—if he does, isn't this our chance? Won't he be handing us an alibi on a plate . . .? And what had you to lose? If he didn't come, and you were proved to be mistaken, you would have sacrificed one night of bliss. But the possible gain was enormous—freedom and a fortune for you and your lover . . . So through Saturday you worked out a contingency plan, which went into action after Quarry's Saturday night phone call from the hotel . . .

'Your plans for disposing of the body and establishing the alibi were not, of course, thought up in a few hectic minutes. How could they be? They were prepared beforehand in careful detail. Saxon's night arrangements—the hurriedly organized theatre visit and the meal in the restaurant—were to cover the period when otherwise he might conceivably have been travelling to the hotel. You provided in good time the material for the confusing dispositions at the track, having had plenty of opportunity to study the copy of the *Lowark Advertiser* that Driscoll sent to your husband . . .

'So there it was—you had your plan, you were all set for the eventuality. You had no fears, or doubts about complications, since you had no knowledge of Quarry's *own* alibi plans, or of his intention to kill you . . .

'Saxon's story that he acted in self-defence was, of course, pathetic nonsense. There was no intruder. There was no tackling of a man with a gun. There was no struggle. Nothing that Saxon said was true. His late arrival here was for alibi purposes, not out of caution about neighbours. He came here all prepared for action—in old clothes, which could be discarded if by chance they became bloodstained. He came with gloves, which he wore through the night—hence the smudging of most of Quarry's fingerprints on the wheel of the Rover ...

'When, after the murder, it was realized that my inquiries were turning away from a possible factory motive to a more personal one, and getting too near for comfort, someone wrote and posted an anonymous letter to me. I imagine it was you who suggested it. You knew, of course, that John Driscoll had no alibi for that night. You also knew that Quarry had spoken on the phone to Betty Driscoll—which would have appeared to give him the opportunity to make an assignation. Since you were well known in Lowark, I imagine it was Saxon who drove there to post the letter. We shall probably find that on the relevant afternoon he was away from his office, ostensibly talking to a client ...

'I don't know, naturally, just what happened at the killing. Since Quarry was so much stronger than Saxon, I would guess there was an ambush. I see Saxon waiting in the dark beside the drive—perhaps in that summer-house—listening for Quarry's car, for the quiet approach on foot. Then a quick step out, a blow on the back of the head with the sandbag you'd provided, more blows to produce unconsciousness—and deliberate murder ...'

Burns paused, eyeing the terrified and speechless girl on the settee. Her hands covered her face—she was trembling ...

'Mrs Quarry,' he said, 'you have shown yourself to be a cruel and conscienceless woman. Saxon may have struck the blows, but you stood by and watched your husband being brutally beaten down and stamped on and choked to death when he was helpless. I see Saxon as a weak man, seduced by your attractions. I see you as an unscrupulous and calculating plotter, who thought up this wicked plan, who instigated it, who drove Saxon on ...'

'*Stop*!' Alma cried. 'Stop!—it's not true. He suggested everything ...'

Ryder gave a long sigh, and switched off the tape-recorder.

Burns went to the door. 'Bring Saxon in,' he called. He waited impatiently. The girl's sobs were genuine enough now—and distracting. In a moment Saxon came in, with Williams close behind him.

'Peter Saxon,' Burns said, 'I now arrest you for the wilful murder of Robert Quarry. Alma Quarry, I now arrest you for complicity in the murder of your husband . . . Right, let's get them down to the station.'

Chapter Two

It was a few minutes before midnight. The three detectives were back at their Lowark headquarters, having a beer together in the canteen at the end of their long day.

Constable Williams said, 'you didn't really believe all that, sir, did you? About the woman having instigated it all?'

Burns shook his head. 'No, Constable, I didn't. Saxon was obviously the dominant character—you could tell by the way he answered for her all the time. It just seemed the most promising way of provoking her to say something she shouldn't.'

'It worked like a miracle,' Ryder said. 'Though I'm not sure you didn't stretch some of the rules a bit, sir.'

'If a man can't stretch the rules on his retirement night, Sergeant, I'd like to know when he can. I think you'll find the trial judge will allow the record to be put in. Even if he doesn't, the facts are all there now. It's a watertight case.'

'Personally,' Ryder said, 'I'd apportion the blame about fifty-fifty between them. He was a cold-blooded villain—but she was a beautiful rattlesnake . . . Not a very edifying case for your last one, sir.'

Burns shrugged. 'We're not paid to be edified—we're paid to bring rogues to book. I've found it a worthwhile job. I'm satisfied.'

'I've no complaints,' Ryder said. He drank—and pondered. 'I'm still a bit puzzled about how Quarry was going to deal with the situation if he'd found them together. How was he going to kill them?'

'With his hands, I'd guess. An ex-commando . . . He'd have chopped Saxon down in a moment. And probably strangled his wife—that's what they mostly do. In the mood he'd have been in, I'd say the whole job would have taken him about sixty seconds flat.'

'He'd have had to do something about the bodies,' Ryder said. 'Even *his* alibi wouldn't have been too safe if his wife and her lover had been found murdered in his own home.'

He'd have arranged things, I'm sure. A forced window—an assumed break-in—a few objects stolen—Alma dead in her bed . . . Saxon's body found a week later, maybe, in some wood fifty miles to the north. No personal connection suspected between the two victims . . . He'd have got away with it.'

'What would he have done if he'd found Alma innocently asleep, and no one else there?'

'Slipped quietly away, I suppose . . . Or into bed with her! That's something we'll never know.'

Burns glanced at his watch. It was a minute past midnight. 'Well,' he said, 'I'm a civilian now. Mr Willams, it's been a pleasure to know you . . . Tom, you can slap me on the back and call me Joe . . .'

Chapter Three

The dormobile stood loaded in the drive. Burns, looking somewhat peculiar in a bright check shirt and a deerstalker hat, was studying the route to Dover. Alice was going round the house, making sure the windows were all shut.

A car drew up and Ryder got out. He had a flat brown-paper parcel under his arm.

'Morning, sir,' he said. 'Ready for off?'

'Just about, Tom.'

'I've been asked by some of the lads to give you this, sir. There was to have been a proper presentation, but the case got in the way . . . A small token of affection and esteem!'

Burns called, 'Alice!' In a moment, his wife joined him. 'A going-away present,' he said. 'You open it.'

Alice undid the parcel. It contained a framed photograph. The photograph showed a portly Burns, struggling in a street with three long-haired youths against a background of placards and slogans. Underneath the picture there was a written caption: WHO SAID A POLICEMAN'S LOT IS NOT A HIPPY ONE?

Burns gave a reminiscent smile. He remembered the demo very well. He shouldn't have been involved at all—not at his age, and in plain clothes. But a uniformed constable had been on the ground—so he'd joined in.

'I like it,' he said. 'I like it very much . . . Tell the lads Alice and I will treasure it.'

Alice got into the van, holding the photograph in her lap. Burns squeezed in behind the wheel.

Ryder said, with a sidelong glance at Alice, 'Well, sir, if you should happen to change your mind about your retirement plans, I'm sure there'll always be a Securicor job available.'

Burns shook his head. 'Not for me, Tom. I'm retiring for good. If this trip works out, Alice and I plan to get a van of our own and just cruise around in warm places—don't we, dear? I shall sit on grassy river banks, watching the pools, working out which way the fish are likely to go and the best bait to catch them with . . .'

Ryder grinned. 'That's not retirement, sir. That's just going on with the job!'

www.ingramcontent.com/pod-product-compliance
Ingram Content Group UK Ltd.
Pitfield, Milton Keynes, MK11 3LW, UK
UKHW040104010325
455690UK00002B/11